STRANGER IN THE WOODS

STRANGER
IN THE
WOODS

A Hattie Farwell Mystery

Betty Orlemann

Red Anvil Press

This is a work of fiction. Any resemblance of the characters to persons living or dead is purely coincidental.

RED ANVIL PRESS

1393 Old Homestead Drive, Second floor
Oakland, Oregon 97462—9506.
E MAIL: editor@elderberrypress. com
TEL/FAX: 541. 459. 6043
www. elderberrypress. com

RED ANVIL books are available from your favorite bookstore, amazon. com, or from our 24 hour order line: 1. 800. 431. 1579

Library of Congress Control Number: 2003112876
Publisher's Catalog—in—Publication Data
Stranger in the Woods / Betty Orlemann
ISBN 19308597813
1. Murder—Fiction.
2. Mystery—Fiction.
3. Detective—Fiction.
4. Politics—Fiction.
5. Murder Mystery—Fiction.
I. Title

This book was written, printed and bound in the United States of America.

This book is dedicated to my three children
and their spouses:
Duff and Kim, Dick and Karen and Joan and Glenn.
It is also dedicated to the memory of our
little daughter, Connie.

Betty Orlemann

chapter one

*H*attie Farwell, dressed as usual in a long
black skirt, white blouse, black boots, and in this case a black cape
because the day was chilly, joined the crowd going up the aisle after
the 11 am service. At the door of the church she shook hands with
the minister then walked briskly across the stone driveway into the
cemetery.

She carried with her two large bouquets of red and white chry-
santhemums which she had placed on the altar in memory of her
brother Fred's birthday. He had been killed during the Second World
War while serving in the Air Force in Europe. So young, she thought.

When she reached his grave she straightened the small Ameri-
can flag in its bronze veterans' holder in front of his gravestone and
placed one of the bouquets next to it. She stared at the inscription

on the stone and marveled that it would have been Fred's 77th birthday that day. After all of these years she still missed him and wondered what he would have done with his life if he had been spared
to come home alive.

Next to Fred's grave were those of her parents and next to them
an empty plot for her. She scattered some of the flowers on their
graves and considered for the thousandth time how her life would
have been different if Fred had lived.

She wasn't bitter, but she remembered that her plans to teach in
Philadelphia were cut short after Fred was killed. Her father became terminally ill and she had to go home to Bucks County to
help her ailing mother with their dairy farm. And now her mother
was long gone, and Hattie, at 80-years of age, was still living in the
home in which she and Fred had been born and raised — the fourth
generation on that land and in that house.

She carried the second bouquet a few paces across the grass to
another grave — that of her best and life-long friend Annie Turner
and placed them tenderly in front of her gravestone. "Oh, Annie,
Annie," she whispered, "How I miss you."

The first signs of spring were barely in the air that late February
day, and Hattie shivered a little as she thought of Annie who had
been deliberately killed by a hit-run driver in Philadelphia in November. Although the murderer had been caught with Hattie's help,
she took small comfort from that fact. With a deep sigh she walked
to her car.

As she was driving from the cemetery Hattie saw a small old
man step from an ancient pickup truck at the end of the driveway.
Carrying a little bunch of spring flowers he walked slowly across the
lawn between the graves. She didn't recognize him, and that was
unusual as she knew just about everyone in that part of Plumstead
Township. Or at least she did before the recent rash of development.

However, from his appearance it was highly unlikely that he
had moved into one of those new glamorous and expensive homes.
Hattie slowed her car to a stop, her eyes following the stranger. She
allowed a slight frown to crease her forehead as she saw him make

his slow way to an almost forgotten corner of the graveyard where he knelt at the side of one of the graves and laid the flowers by the headstone.

Apparently he was praying, and Hattie feeling that she was intruding, quickly drove away. There was no one else in sight.

The little man was praying, his knees indenting the cold damp earth. "I miss you so, m'darlin. You'll never know," he sobbed with tears coursing down his wrinkled cheeks. Mindless of the dampness he knelt silently a while before he started to push himself stiffly to his feet.

He never heard nor saw the bearded man who sneaked up behind him. He did not feel the blow on his head which knocked him into unconsciousness. Nor did he feel the powerful fingers which encircled his neck and squeezed the life from his body.

His attacker laughed out loud, "There will be more!" he exclaimed. The man, six feet three inches tall with a strong, muscular build, adjusted a black knit cap on his thick gray hair and effortlessly lifted the slight body of his victim into his arms. "You helped ruin my life, and and now I've taken yours!" he gloated.

He carried the old man's limp body to a deep ditch at the side of the cemetery and dumped it in after searching the pockets. Then he carefully covered it with piles of dead leaves.

Using the old man's keys the killer drove the ancient pickup truck deep into the woods bordering the cemetery. He removed the license plate before returning to his own old pick-up truck which he had parked along the side of the road.

chapter two

*H*attie's home was less than two miles from the church. She drove into her private lane and parked between the house and the barn. As always she crossed the porch and opened the door into her kitchen — by far her favorite room in the house.

It was a big square room with a large walk-in fireplace in the wall facing the door. A round oak table stood in the center of the room with old chairs surrounding it and an antique lamp hanging from open beams above it. She felt herself relax as she walked in. She slipped off her cape and hung it by the door. There's no place like home, she thought.

A rhythmic thump-thump-thump greeted her, and she laughed as her enormous gray Irish Wolf hound/wolf mix expressed with wagging tail his delight at seeing her home again.

"Lazy Wolf!" she chided, "Can't you even stand up when I come in?"

She smiled fondly at the great dog who still remained lying comfortably on his side.

"Are you hungry?" she asked him, and he wagged his tail even harder.

She took a large dog bone from a container on the counter and threw it to him. Without getting up he swiveled his head around until he could slide the bone into his mouth with the aid of his long pink tongue.

Hattie took a gold and white homespun table cloth from a drawer next to the sink, unfolded it and spread it over the oak table — all to the accompaniment of Wolf's loud chewing. She smiled and shook her head.

She put water on to boil for tea and made herself an egg salad sandwich while she waited. When she sat down to eat she wondered about the old man in the cemetery.

Who is he? she pondered. Where did he come from? He must have been cold with such a thin coat and no hat to cover his balding head.

"Perhaps I'll go back and see whose grave he was kneeling next to," she said aloud. Wolf banged his tail against the floor again when she spoke. She smiled at him, "And perhaps I'd better take you for a walk first," she added.

At those magic words Wolf pulled himself to a standing position and panting in expectation he walked to Hattie's side.

She removed her cape from its peg by the door and paused for a moment to glance into a mirror hanging next to it. She saw a plain old woman with with gray eyes and gray hair, some strands of which had escaped from the bun at the nape of her neck. She decided to ignore them. Who am I going to see anyway? she thought.

As soon as she opened the door, Wolf bolted out and ran across the porch. He jumped down over its three steps and trotted happily along the flagstone path, through the open gate and onto the lane where he turned to wait for Hattie.

"This time, boy, I want to walk up the lane to the new development," she stated. Could the dog really understand her? she wondered as the huge animal turned and started to trot up the lane.

Her parents, grandparents and great grandparents had a great reverence for the land, and by the time she and Fred were born they had accumulated almost 300 acres. That was a fact for which she was grateful when she had been forced to sell the 100 acre pasture at the top of the lane. She had given the 100 acre woods across the lane from her house to the Heritage Conservancy to be preserved in perpetuity. Now her house and barn stood on the remaining 100 acres which she intended to will to the Conservancy.

When she strolled away from her house past the large red barn and the silo next to it she was overcome with nostalgia. She could almost imagine the lowing of the cows. She could remember so well the way they wandered up to the pasture on the cow path their ancestors had created. That cow path was now just a dirt lane turning and twisting its way up the hill through a cedar forest.

She could remember the land before the cedar trees had grown there. Just fields of hay, alfalfa and corn. Fields which once neglected had grown the cedars.

Wolf ran off between the trees. Hattie could hear him crashing through the undergrowth. Every so often she caught a glimpse of him as he explored the woods. She knew that before long he would come back to her, and he soon appeared on the lane in front of her, panting happily.

She rounded the last bend in the lane and came out at the new development. Hattie hadn't walked up there in several months and was astounded at the amount of work that had been finished during her absence.

The lane led to a rutted road which was dotted on either side by Victorian-type houses. Each had a porch in front and most had gabled roofs and bay windows. She turned right onto the road and saw that many of the houses in that area were painted in Victorian golds, tans, reds and greens once again so popular.

Unlike the originals, these houses had attached garages, but the designer had been clever enough to plan them so that the doors opened to the side and not the front as in the case of so many development homes. To her surprise Hattie found the houses homey and attractive — especially the ones on the right hand side of the road whose roomy rear yards backed up to her woods.

She walked farther down the road which was paved at that point. She noticed one solitary "sold" sign on the right. The others didn't seem quite ready for occupancy yet. She decided to come back in a week or two to greet her new neighbors.

Before she could walk farther a cold wind blew up and the sky filled with dark clouds. Rain is coming, she guessed, and she turned and started home. "Come Wolf," she called, and the dog abandoned his investigation of the neighborhood and ran home ahead of her.

Just as they reached Hattie's house great drops of rain started pelting the roof.

The rain continued for the rest of the week thereby discouraging any plans Hattie had wanted to make about visiting the cemetery, or for that matter welcoming her new neighbors in the development. Oh well, she thought philosophically, no one is going to leave the cemetery, and the new people will probably not move in while its raining.

Nothing of note happened during the week. Hattie simply relaxed each day and read her morning paper in her rocking chair in front of the fire before puttering around the house with a dust rag and vacuum cleaner or reading a book or writing letters or paying bills. No matter, she was content.

On Friday she read and reread an article in the paper about a Doylestown woman whose body had been found in the trunk of her car the day before. A shopper had reported a bad smell coming from the trunk of the car parked in the lot of the Montgomeryville Mall.

The woman had been hit in the neck and strangled. The police had identified her from her fingerprints as Marla Coulton, 36, a newlywed. She was a guidance counselor in a local high school, and according to the people who had been interviewed, she was popular with students and teachers alike. Other than her husband she had no other close relatives. Her husband had reported her missing three days earlier, the paper said.

Hattie shivered slightly. "That's too close to home," she said aloud, "and anyway, I've had enough of murders." Wolf banged his tail against the floor.

The rain finally stopped on Saturday night, and although the ground was muddy and soggy, Sunday dawned warm and beautiful.

Hattie attended church as usual and afterward strolled through the cemetery. The flowers she had left on the graves the week before were scattered about and sadly droopy. She scooped them up and walked to the ditch next to the graveyard where the custodian routinely dumped leaves and dead flowers from the graves.

She dropped the flowers into the ditch and noticed that the wind and rain had stirred up the leaves in it. She was about to go to the grave where the little man had been kneeling the week before, when she suddenly noticed a hand poking out of the leaves.

"Oh, Good Heavens!" she cried. For a moment she stared at the hand in disbelief, then turned and hurried to her car as fast as she could. Once home, she raced into her kitchen and ran to the phone to call the police.

She was pleased when the officer who answered the phone was Lt. Jim Sawyer, an old friend who had helped solve the murder mysteries last November.

Hattie spoke too rapidly in her excitement and had to slow down so that Jim could understand what she was saying. "Jim," she began, "Thank Heaven it's you! I've just come home from church. There is a hand protruding from the leaves in the ditch next to the cemetery!"

"Can you meet me there right away?" he asked calmly, "I want you to show me exactly where this hand is." She agreed and they both hung up, but before the phones disconnected she could have sworn she heard him utter, "Oh no! Not again!"

Although Hattie's home was much closer to the cemetery than police headquarters was, Jim Sawyer arrived at almost the same time she did. After they both parked their cars she led him hurriedly between gravestones until they reached the ditch.

"There!" she said breathlessly, "There's the hand!"

"Oh-my-gosh!" he ejaculated, "You're right!"

And with that he jumped into the ditch and gently scraped away the soggy leaves. To Hattie's horror he uncovered the body of the little man whom she had watched the week before.

Leaving the body alone, Jim used his radio to contact the coroner, and then they began to wait.

"Have you seen this man before Miss Hattie?" he asked

Hattie told him about the previous Sunday when the sad little man came to the cemetery. "I was about to check the gravestone where he knelt when I saw his hand," she said, "Come, let's see whom he came to see." "Her name was Mary Delaney Tierney," Jim said as he read the inscription on the marble tombstone. "She died five years ago."

"She was 80 at the time of her death." Hattie said as she, too, read the inscription over Jim's shoulder. "I'd say that she was obviously the little man's wife."

"Look," said Jim, "Look at this tombstone next to Mary's. It has 'Timothy Tierney' impressed in it with just the date of his birth. No death date. I suppose we can assume that the body in the ditch is Timothy Tierney's. He would be 87. That seems right."

"Yes," said Hattie, "Pretty soon we'll know the death date, too. Poor little man. I can only imagine that he was murdered last Sunday."

" Was he Timothy Tierney? Why did he want to be buried here? Who killed him and why? You didn't recognize him. I wonder if anyone did." Jim was clearly perplexed. "We'll know soon enough, I'm sure. It's a lucky thing that you saw him last Sunday, Miss Hattie. You've made my job a lot easier." He smiled his charming smile at her and she could do nothing but smile back.

"By the way, Did you see how the man got here? Did someone bring him or did he have his own car?" Jim asked.

"Oh my!" Hattie stated, "How stupid of me! He had a little old pick-up truck. I'm not even sure of the color, but it was a dark shade. Anyway, he parked it near the gate."

"Hmm," mumbled Jim, "I wonder what happened to it."

The coroner arrived just then with a police investigator and a detective from the District Attorney's office. Soon they had yellow police tape across the ditch where the body was found as well as around the burial plot. Hattie knew that her presence there was not needed so she left the four men and went home, her brain full of questions about the deaths of Timothy Tierney and Marla Coulton.

Was there a connection between them? It seemed unlikely. Was there a serial killer on the loose?

An hour later Jim came to her door. "We found an old pick-up truck hidden way back in the woods," he told her. The license had been removed, and there was no kind of identification in the truck so we'll have to wait until the PIN number has been researched.

"I'd be willing to bet, though, that the truck was Timothy Tierney's, but would you come look at it to see if it's the one you saw last Sunday?"

"I'd be glad to," said Hattie, "How about fingerprints?" she asked, "Were there any at all?"

"None. Everything was wiped clean," he answered with a sigh. "I did find out something else, though. Timothy Tierney's uncle had been caretaker at the church for a number of years. His name was Pat Moore.

"Anyway, he had no children, and for some reason he left Timothy and his wife two grave sites in his plot when he died. You'll see his grave next to Mary's. Maybe he didn't want to be lonely."

"Well for Heaven's sakes!" exclaimed Hattie, "I remember Pat. He was around for years. A very nice man. But that doesn't answer my question about what connection Timothy had with Marla Coulton.

"No, not at all," said Jim, "Maybe there wasn't any."

chapter three

*T*he following morning Hattie awakened at 5:45 when she heard the car of her newspaper delivery man stop by her gate. Seconds later she heard the "thump" of the paper landing on her kitchen porch.

She rose immediately, shoved her feet into her well-worn bedroom slippers, took her blue flannel bathrobe from the closet, and still pulling it around her, she hurried down the winding stairs from her room to the kitchen below. Wolf greeted her as she opened the door at the bottom of the stairs. His yellow eyes gleamed in anticipation of a trip outside, and his great tail wagged furiously. She took a brief moment to hug him before she started across the room.

He jogged happily back and forth between Hattie and the door, taking five steps to each one of hers until she finally slipped the bolt to unlock the door and let him out. She watched him dash across the porch, jump the steps as usual and race down the path, through the open gate and across the lane into the woods.

Hattie leaned over a trifle stiffly and scooped up the paper. She unfolded it quickly and saw the heading, "MURDER REPORTED IN PLUMSTEAD." As anxious as she was to read the story, she forced herself to wait while she made coffee and started a fire.

Once comfortable in her rocking chair by the fireplace, a fire burning cheerfully on the hearth and a cup of steaming coffee on the table next to her, Hattie began to read the paper:

"Plumstead Township Police are seeking help in identifying the body of an elderly man which was found in a ditch next to Saint Matthew's Cemetery yesterday. According to the coroner, Dr. Hugh Plaski, the man had been dead for about a week. Plaski stated that the man had been struck on the head with some kind of blunt in-strument and then strangled."

The article went on to describe the murder of School Guidance Counselor Marla Coulton whose body was found on Friday. "The two murders," according to the paper, "were similar. Both victims had been struck before being strangled. However, a connection be-tween the victims is yet to be found. No weapons were found in either case police said."

That's funny, Hattie thought, I wonder why Timothy Tierney's name was not released. I guess they had good reason, she mused with a slight frown.

As she continued to read through the paper, she stopped short when she reached a real estate ad. It featured a photograph of a good looking family of four under a heading which read, "FIRST FAMILY MOVES INTO BROOKSIDE FARMS." Although the first names were not used the feature told how Mr. and Mrs. Atkins had realized their dream when they and their two little girls moved into their beautiful Victorian-type home at 57 Running Brook Circle in Brookside Farms, Plumstead Township, less than a week ago.

Other than saying that the family had moved from Middletown Township, Hattie was disappointed to see that very little else was written about them. The rest of the article was devoted to a glowing report of the house, its price and that of the other 34 homes in the neighborhood (many still under construction), and the size of the lots (from 1/2 to 3/4 acres each).

She was interested to see that each home had wall to wall carpeting, a side entry two car garage, a 20 by 16 foot family room, four bedrooms, 2 1/2 baths, a fireplace in the family room, a living room and dining room and a full basement and central air conditioning.

The article went on and on, and Hattie became bored with the flowery descriptions. She ripped the article out, folded the paper and put it down. I must get up to meet the Atkins very soon, she thought.

Hattie wasn't the only one to take an interest in that ad. A big bearded man with gray hair mostly hidden beneath a knit cap, sat in his old pick-up truck in a parking lot in Bristol Township and gazed at the picture with delight, "So your name is Atkins now," he said with a smile. I'll be paying you a visit very soon!"

The subjects of their interest were happily oblivious to the attention the article had drawn.

chapter four

*T*he bearded man started the engine of his old pick-up truck and drove north to Upper Bucks County. His plans were going even better than he had planned, and he was feeling extremely self-congratulatory.

Yellow teeth gleamed through his beard when he smiled. Mrs. Atkins, is it? Donna Atkins. I'll be keeping an eye on you, Donna Atkins. "I'm off to 57 Running Brook Circle in Brookside Farms," he sang off key.

He smiled as he thought of his accomplishments. Timothy Tierney had been a cinch. That little old guy couldn't put up any kind of fight. There was only one fly in the ointment. He thought no one would find Timothy's body. He really hoped no one would find any of the bodies, but that didn't happen.

Maybe it was better that they were found. Marla Coulton was pretty easy, too. He followed her to the mall after school on Monday a week ago. He had watched her open her trunk to put her packages in, karate chopped the back of her neck knocking her out and strangled her. Then he dumped her body into the trunk and left her there.

He recalled with pleasure waiting until 2 o'clock Friday morning to attack his third victim. As he sat in his truck in the Falls Township parking lot of Sam's Bar and Grill he almost salivated with the excitement of his anticipated third kill.

Timothy's and Marla's bodies had not yet been found, and that fact made him almost manic with joy. "This one won't be found either," he crowed.

A freezing rain was falling, and he was getting very cold. He wanted to start his engine in order to use the heater, but he was afraid of attracting attention. He rubbed his arms and hugged himself through his thick jacket.

He remembered keeping his eyes on the door of the tavern. Suddenly it swung open and a shaft of light illuminated the dark surface of the parking lot. He jumped in spite of himself, but it was only a man who lurched across the pavement singing to himself drunkenly. The man staggered to the road and disappeared in the rainy darkness.

He became agitated and restless, "Where the hell is she?" he remembered mumbling to himself. He had seen her go in to start her shift at six. It was almost quarter after two, and she still hadn't come out. It made him nervous just to remember.

Finally he saw her. She turned out the lights, opened the door and locked it behind her. He moved quickly to hide behind her car while she walked into the nearly deserted parking lot and started toward her 1982 shiny red Chevy coupe.

He recalled seeing her look uneasily at his truck and then start to run. By the time she realized that he was crouched behind her car it was too late.

He was happy with his memory of removing her keys and wallet from her purse and dumping her strangled lifeless body into her trunk. As he had preplanned he drove her car to Van Sciver Lake and buried Tanya Williams' corpse under a large pile of debris beneath the railroad track bridge.

He then had driven her car to a cluttered automobile graveyard from which he walked back to his own truck.

"I do nice work," he congratulated himself. "And now I'm off to see Donna!"

chapter five

oft music on the clock radio awakened Donna Atkins from a sound sleep. She stretched comfortably and turned onto her back.

When she forced her eyes open and looked at the clock, its glowing digital figures showed her it was 5:45 — 45 minutes before she usually woke up. She was not surprised to see that her husband, Ben, was no longer in his side of the bed.

The sound of rushing water coming from their bathroom told her that Ben was about to take a shower. She briefly considered joining him under the steaming spray, but changed her mind somewhat reluctantly when she remembered that he had to start out early on a long business trip and couldn't afford any delays.

She flung a pink flannel robe over her flowered cotton nightgown, thrust her feet into fuzzy bright red slippers, reached into the foggy bathroom for her comb, toothbrush, washcloth and towel and ran downstairs to the powder room to make stabs at facing the day.

Minutes later she was in the kitchen brewing a pot of coffee. She attempted to look outside, but it was still too dark to see anything but her own reflection in the window.

She grimaced at her image. Although it was slightly distorted, she could see straight light brown hair hanging next to a face which, without make-up, she believed looked older than her 35 years.

Ben joined her as she was scooping his scrambled eggs onto his plate. He took the plate and two pieces of toast from the toaster as they popped up and sat at his usual place at the counter which separated the kitchen from the family room. She brought over two cups of black coffee and sat next to him, sipping hers but not yet eating anything.

She watched him over the rim of her cup as he reached to turn on the radio. "He's even better looking now than he was 11 years ago when we were married," she thought.

She approved of his taste in clothing, gray flannel slacks with a sharp crease, highly polished brown loafers, light blue shirt, regimental navy, red and light blue striped tie, and she admired the way his navy sport coat fit over his broad shoulders.

His dark brown hair was receding a bit at the temples, but it still held the soft waves which had appealed to her so much when they met. "At 38 he's handsomer than ever," she thought, "It's not fair."

She started to tell him to drive carefully on the long drive from Bucks County across the state to Pittsburgh, but he held up his hand for silence as the newscaster's voice boomed into the room.

"In Bucks County, Falls Township police report the discovery of the body of a woman buried beneath debris under the Conrail line near Van Sciver Lake. The body, which appears to have been dead about two days, was discovered by two teenagers last night.

"According to police the woman was strangled. She has yet to be identified." said the announcer in bright tones. "Police are checking reports of missing persons and a dental check will be performed later today when the body is autopsied.

"This is the third body found in Bucks County in the past week. Police refuse to speculate as to whether or not a serial killer might be on the loose," continued the announcer, his voice still chipper, "However," he said, "at this point it would seem likely as all of the victims were knocked unconscious before being strangled.

"The body of an elderly man was found Sunday morning at Saint Matthews Cemetery in Plumstead Township. It was buried beneath leaves in a ditch next to the cemetery. No further information will be released until the bodies have been identified and the next of kin notified.

"Another body found murdered last week in Montgomeryville was identified as that of Marla Coulton, 36, of Doylestown."

Ben's hazel eyes registered alarm, "Make sure you lock all of the doors all of the time," he instructed, "You know how careless you can be."

Donna suppressed a smile. "Donna," Ben continued firmly, "We are really isolated here. Please, be careful. I'll worry about you and the girls the whole time I'm gone."

Donna knew he was right. She had to admit that she would be happier when more people moved into their development.

She hopped down from her stool and walked to a pair of sliding glass doors in the back wall of the family room. No one had bothered to close the curtains the night before, no one ever did, "Who would possibly be around to look in?" she thought.

She hid her momentary uneasiness with a small chuckle. The day was beginning to brighten. She looked through the doors across a patio and 50 feet of dark lawn to the silhouettes of the Cedar trees in the woods beyond. One reason they had purchased this house was the view of the woods, almost 100 acres of them, and the promise that they would remain undeveloped forever.

She turned and watched Ben spread strawberry jam on his second piece of toast, "Do you want anything else?" she asked.

He looked her up and down with a sexy leer on his face. "Besides that!" she exclaimed, and they both laughed.

Finishing his toast in two quick bites, he stepped down from his stool and strode toward her. Even after all these years his nearness excited her.

Although she was five feet six inches tall and weighed 130 pounds, she felt dwarfed by Ben who was six feet four and weighed 210 pounds. He grabbed her into his arms and kissed her soundly.

And then, with one quick movement, he reached down to the hems of her gown and robe and pulled them up to her neck exposing her entire body. She wriggled in protest and attempted to reclaim her clothing.

He laughed but refused to release her. His hands explored her body. "You have such nice things to play with," he murmured into her left ear.

"The window!" she gasped as she continued fruitlessly to try to free herself.

"Who would possibly be around to look in?" he mimicked her.

"The girls!" she squealed, "What if one of the girls came in?"

"Mindy and Melanie are just like their mother," he laughed again, "They would sleep all morning if they could." He continued exploring her nakedness.

Defeated she threw her arms around his neck and kissed him. "I love you so much," she whispered, "I'm really going to miss you."

"Me, too," he breathed into her hair. He released her gown and robe and gave an exaggerated sigh as he watched them flutter to the floor. "Gotta go," he said, "See you about dinner time on Friday."

To her surprise tears gathered in her blue eyes, "I should be used to your trips by now, but I always hate to see you go," she said with an apologetic smile. "You'll be home in four days, you'd think it was four weeks the way I'm carrying on!" She grabbed a tissue from her pocket and blew her nose as he picked up his sample case and suitcase.

Ben looked at her seriously for a moment. "You know," he stated, "You haven't left this house except to buy food since we moved in last week. Don't you think it would be a good idea to look for a part time job? You should get to know people — do something besides cleaning and being with the girls.

"You have your degree in early childhood education. I saw a job advertised in yesterday's paper for an assistant preschool teacher at that little church over on the pike.

Why don't you see if there is still an opening? It would be ideal, because you could still be home when the girls are out of school." His voice was firm.

She said nothing, but she knew he was right. Nonetheless she really liked being home, unpacking, puttering around and doing what she felt like doing.

She hoped she wasn't becoming a recluse or falling victim to some awful phobia. Maybe she should shake herself into some kind of action after all.

Giving her a final hug, he unlocked the deadbolt on the door to the garage on the far side of the family room and stepped out. She stood in the doorway and watched as he used the remote control and the garage doors slid up.

He started his car, they waved to each other, he backed out, the doors rumbled shut, and he was gone.

It was 6 o'clock when she reentered the kitchen to pour herself a second cup of coffee. Sipping it she looked absently through the window over the sink and stiffened. Had she seen something move out there in the woods?

"How fanciful of me," she thought, "If there is anything out there it's only a deer." Her sense of humor got the better of her and she laughed out loud, "I must have looked a sight - framed in that doorway with my nightclothes around my neck and nothing else on except those bright red fuzzy slippers! — I hope it was only a deer!"

An hour later she had made their bed and started a load of wash in the basement laundry but was still in her nightgown and robe. She climbed the stairs to the second floor and walked into her daughters' room where she found them both, as predicted by their father, sound asleep in their twin beds.

Nine year-old Mindy had one arm resting over "Pal" her black cat. The cat's head rested on the pillow next to Mindy's and his eyes were shut tight

They had been living in the county's Middletown Township when four years ago Mindy had found "Pal", a tiny stray kitten, in a lot near their rented home. Although the whole family loved the cat, there was no doubt that Mindy was his favorite.

Donna leaned over, kissed Mindy's cheek and brushed her dark, wavy hair away from her face. "Time to get up, sleepy head," she said softly.

"Oh, is it Monday already? Mindy groaned. She rolled over grudgingly, pushed away her covers and smiled a smile very like her father's, "Morning, Mommy," she said sweetly, her hazel eyes shining.

Six year-old Melanie woke up by herself when she heard her sister talking. They both raced for the bathroom in the hall, "I wanna take the first shower," called Melanie, her straight blonde hair bouncing on her shoulders.

By 8:25 the girls had dressed, eaten breakfast, brushed their teeth and had put on their coats. They collected their book bags and lunches from an old drop-leaf table in the front hall, and left the house. Donna followed them across the porch and down the walk to wait for their school bus.

"Mom!" exclaimed Mindy in horror, "You can't wait out here dressed like that! All the other kids will laugh! Please, go back in the house! It's bad enough that you are in your nightgown, but those red slippers don't even go!"

Melanie gave her mother a gap toothed grin, "That's O.K., Mommy," she said softly. She could never stand to see anyone hurt, "Anyhow, I gave you those slippers."

Donna laughed and kissed her daughters goodbye, "I'll wait in the doorway out of sight," she promised, "Your friends won't see me."

After the school bus had picked up the girls and rounded a bend in the road to her right, Donna went back outside to retrieve the morning paper from the driveway. As she was turning to go inside again, a dark blue, dirt-smeared pick-up truck drove slowly by coming from her right, the direction in which the bus had gone.

In fact, the truck was so incrusted with dirt that the license number was indiscernible and the windows almost opaque. Donna could barely see the driver, but she had the impression that he wore a knit cap, dark glasses and a beard.

She hoped that the appearance of the truck meant that another house had been sold and the driver was on his way to fix it up for the new owners.

The day was exceptionally warm for late February, and Donna's spirits brightened as she thought of spring and the possibility of neighbors.

She reentered the house through the front door and stepped into the hall, which led back to the family room and kitchen. Through an open arch on the right of the hall was the living room, its windows looking out over the front lawn and the road. There was not a stick of furniture in it. "Living room furniture will have to wait," they had told each other. "The mortgage is much more important."

Across the hall through a matching arch was the dining room. It was furnished with an antique oak table, sideboard and chairs given to her and Ben by his parents as a wedding gift. It shared the same view as the living room as well as a glimpse through white curtains in a bay window of the house next door. A swinging door in the rear led to the kitchen.

The stairway to the second floor started a few feet back from the dining room entrance and shared a common wall with the dining room. The cellar stairs descended beneath the main stairway and were accessed by a door in the hall outside the family room. The cellar door was, as usual, about four inches ajar as a convenience for Pal to get to his litter box on the floor below. The powder room and a coat closet were across the hall from the stairs.

Donna walked back to the kitchen where she opened a can of cat food and gave Pal his breakfast. She then went downstairs to the laundry to put the washed clothes into the drier and returned to the family room where she sat in a recliner with a third cup of coffee, a toasted bagel and the newspaper.

She had to admit that it was good being alone in the house after the frantic pace of getting two children off to school and Ben off to

Pittsburgh.

As much as she would miss Ben, his business trips were almost like vacations for her, she mused. She and the girls would have pizza for dinner one night, maybe go out for hamburgers another, maybe hot dogs another — fun food, no elaborate cooking —they'd eat all the things they loved and Ben hated. "I guess I am getting lazy," she reproached herself.

Pal jumped into her lap and curled up, purring. "Life is so peaceful, though," she thought contentedly as she stroked the cat's sleek fur. She closed her eyes , I don't know why Ben thinks it's so important for me to go back to work.

chapter six

*D*onna awoke with a start when the clock on the mantelpiece above the family room fireplace was striking 10.

The sun was shining brightly through the sliding glass doors, and Pal was stretched out sleeping in a golden patch of light on the floor. The morning paper lay open across her lap and her unfinished coffee sat ice cold on a table next to her chair.

Donna shifted the footrest down and rose quickly, dumping the paper onto the rug. She was a trifle ashamed of herself for being so indolent. She was about to leave the room when she could have sworn she saw a shadow slip away on the patio.

She stepped cautiously to the doors, and concealing herself in the open drape, peeked through a crack between it and the door frame. There was nothing out there but their black-shrouded gas grill.

She retrieved the newspaper from the floor and glanced at the front page which carried no news of the murdered woman. For some reason she was relieved even though she realized that the woman's body must have been found after the paper went to press.

Hoping the assistant teaching position at the local preschool had been filled, she turned to the classified section. At least she could tell Ben she had tried. But she was out of luck, the ad was still running.

Still hoping the job had been taken, she lifted the receiver from a phone on the kitchen counter and dialed the number in the ad. She had only a moment to wait before a soft, sweet voice came on the other end of the line, "Incarnation Preschool."

Donna told the woman, who identified herself as Marge Adams, who she was, that she was answering the ad and what her credentials were. Marge Adams' voice rang with joy when she told Donna to come in at nine o'clock the next morning for an interview.

As she replaced the phone in its cradle, Donna once again thought she saw from the corner of her eye something move across the patio. She shrugged off a sudden chill. It was then that she saw the real estate ad with their picture. She wished it hadn't been published.

"Well, tomorrow I hope I'll have more to occupy my mind than imaginary moving shadows," she said aloud as she ran upstairs to shower and dress.Half an hour later, clad in blue jeans and a white sweatshirt and sneakers, Donna returned to the kitchen where she fixed herself a fried egg sandwich. After eating she placed the breakfast dishes in the dishwasher, ran a sponge over the beige formica counter top, and headed for the laundry to take the clothes from the drier.

Unexpectedly, Pal ran between her feet just as she was starting down the cellar stairs. Donna emitted a startled cry as she pitched forward. Fortunately she was able to grab the handrail forestalling a nasty fall. "If you do that one more time, darn cat, I'll have your head!" she yelled, her heart racing.

Shortly after one o'clock she decided to go for a walk around the neighborhood and see if she could see any signs that a new neighbor might be moving in somewhere nearby. The sound of hammering floated to her from a distance, and she could see men up on the scaffolding of unfinished houses about a block away.

The air smelled like spring, and the sun was delightfully warm. It felt good to be outside as she strolled part way around the circle where she lived and down a couple of adjoining cul de sacs. She admired the different styles and colors of the houses. Even though some were still under construction, the area looked pretty and inviting. She had no doubt that people would soon flock there, "but right now ," she thought, "it feels unreal — like a ghost town."

The area changed abruptly about half way around her circle. The road was no longer paved, and piles of dirt about 20 feet back gave moot testimony that new development was underway. A yellow bulldozer pushed into a pile of earth on what would someday be a front lawn.

There was no sign of the dirty blue pick-up truck, though, nor any sign of a house being readied for occupancy. For some reason she couldn't fathom Donna shivered.

She walked a bit farther on the rutted roadway, and just as she was turning to retrace her steps home, she saw an old dirt lane leading back into the woods. Curious, and ignoring a rusty "PRIVATE ROAD" sign nailed to a tree, she followed it a short distance until she glanced at her watch and realized that it was almost time for the girls' school bus.

When she arrived home she took their mail from the box at the curb and was delighted to find a postcard from South Carolina from her parents who were touring the south in their new recreational vehicle. "Love being retired," they had written. "Will call you Friday night or Saturday when we alight somewhere!"

While she was still standing by the mailbox, the girls school bus pulled up. The children wanted to ride their bikes, but Donna talked them into walking in the woods with her instead. She didn't want to alarm them, but she couldn't bear the thought of letting them out of her sight. It was foolish of her, she thought, but her trepidation was too strong to ignore.

They left the house through the sliding glass doors in the family room and crossed the flagstone patio and the lawn to a path of sorts in the woods. Melanie's blonde ponytail bobbed to and fro as she ran ahead.

They amused themselves by seeing who could find the most signs of spring. "Here are some crocuses," Donna called out.

"Look, the forsythia's starting to come out!" cried Mindy. "Look, look," squealed Melanie, "little green things are growing!"

A gray squirrel chattered at them from a sycamore tree, and songbirds sang unseen from nearby branches.

The path took them up a hill and around a large outcropping of rocks on their left. A tiny brook bubbled gently over its stony course below them on the right.

"I bet that's the brook "Brookside Farms" is named for," Mindy stated, "I've been wondering where it was."

"Why, it just might be at that," Donna agreed. They walked farther into the woods past cedar and pine trees, clumps of rhododendron, damp rocky ledges and a sparse waterfall where the little brook tumbled over a break in the rocks.

Overhead, through the bare branches of deciduous trees, they watched a jet plane leave its white contrail against a clear blue sky.

"I see a robin!" shouted Mindy. "Me, too, me, too!" called Melanie from an unseen spot ahead of them around another bend in the path.

"Who made this path, Mommy?" asked Melanie trotting back to join her and her sister, "Did Daddy make it for us?"

"No, Honey," laughed Donna, "I believe the deer made the path. See, here are some of their hoof prints." The children examined the cloven impressions in the damp earth for a few minutes before continuing their stroll.

Donna followed them, looking absently at the ground from time to time. Suddenly, she was frozen in place as she saw the clear impression of a man's footprint in the center of the path.

"We've gone far enough for today," she called to her daughters, "It's time to turn around and go home." She tried to keep her voice calm. "I'll race you! Last one back has to set the table!" and she started to run, soon letting them pass her.

They did not see a bearded man wearing a knit cap and sunglasses watching them from behind a Cedar thicket.

7

chapter seven

No more than half an hour later Hattie was standing at her mailbox when a dirty blue pick-up truck drove down her lane toward Pike Road. She noticed that the license plate was caked with mud and completely illegible. The windows were so dirty that she had no clear impression of the driver. Like Donna, though, she thought he was big and bearded.

As she pulled her mail from the box she stared after the truck in annoyance. I'll have to put a stop to the workmen using my private lane, she thought. I'll just go up there tomorrow and complain to the foreman.

She was on the second step to her kitchen porch when she heard the phone ringing. It rang two more times before she lifted the receiver. Somewhat breathlessly she answered with her usual cheerful, "hello," and was pleased to hear Jim Sawyer's voice.

"Hi Miss Hattie," he said, "We were correct about the identification of the man in the ditch. He was Timothy Tierney, and he was from Bristol. A woman who owns a florist shop a block from Tierney's home called in response to the newspaper article and told me about this old man who went into her shop every weekend to buy flowers for his wife's grave.

"Apparently the florist was very fond of him, and it was difficult for her to agree to go to the morgue to identify his body. He looked pretty bad as you know, but she identified him positively. Then she began to cry. It took me some time to comfort her. She said that everybody who knew him loved him and added that he had no family."

"Did she have any idea about who would want to kill him?" Hattie asked.

Jim shook his head, "No, none whatsoever. She stated that absolutely no one disliked him."

"How very strange," murmured Hattie, "What about the others? I can't imagine what connection there would be between Marla Coulton, the guidance counselor, and Timothy Tierney. Do you know whether they knew each other?"

"A most unlikely possibility," Jim stated, "An investigation is still underway, but nothing connecting the two has been turned up."

"Then," Hattie mused, "what of the woman's body found in Falls Township? She too was struck on the head and strangled, according to this morning's paper. Have the police identified her body yet? To me it's obvious that all of the victims were killed the same way.

Were their deaths deliberately planned or coincidental? Is there a serial killer on the loose?"

"I wish I could answer your questions, Miss Hattie. You are right, of course, the killings were the same — a very chilling thought. The body in Falls Township has not yet been identified, but she has been dead the better part of a week, according to the coroner - he believes five days. An artist's sketch will be published tomorrow, and I hope someone will come forward with information about her."

"Did the coroner give an estimate as to her age?" Hattie asked.

"As a matter of fact, he did," Jim responded, "He believes that she was about 48. She was five feet two, weighed 118 pounds and had bleached blond hair. That will all be published tomorrow and on T.V. tonight. She had no alcohol or drugs in her system. No one has reported her missing."

"If it is a serial killer, he certainly gets around, doesn't he? One in Upper Bucks, One in Middle Bucks and one in Lower Bucks. Is that significant? Will there be another? If so, where? And more importantly, Why?"

"I don't know, Miss Hattie, but we're looking into it," he chuckled into the phone, "You sure do ask good questions! Well, I've gotta go. I'll be in touch soon. And by the way, make sure you keep your doors locked."

chapter eight

*A*s the carefully calculated last one back, Donna had to set the table as the girls reminded her. However, before she did anything else and as soon as they were all safely inside, she carefully slid the glass doors shut and locked them together. She then pressed the foot locks down behind both doors and pulled the drapes closed.

"How come you closed the drapes, Mommy?" asked Mindy, "You never did that before."

Before Donna could come up with an excuse, she was saved by the ringing of the phone. She glanced at the clock. It was only 4:30.

"Hi!" it was Ben's voice. His trip had been uneventful if long. He had met with one of his customers and was dressing for dinner with another. Everything was fine, but how was everything at home?

She hoped she sounded normal and casual enough when she said brightly, "Oh, just great, except that we miss you." He seemed satisfied, and she changed the subject, "You'll be happy to know that I have an appointment for an interview at Incarnation Preschool tomorrow morning," she told him. He said he was delighted. The girls chatted with him for a few minutes, and Donna was a trifle relieved when he hung up.

After a dinner of hamburgers, French fries and applesauce, she helped Mindy with her math homework, listened to Melanie read a story and tucked them both into bed early over their loud protests.

"I *am* nine years old!" protested Mindy, "Why do I have to be treated like a six year-old baby?"

"BABY?" shrieked Melanie, "I am *not a baby!*" And she burst into tears.

The danger in the woods, imagined or otherwise, was forgotten by Donna as she calmed her little girls, heard their prayers and kissed them good night. As usual Pal settled himself next to Mindy for the night.

The following morning Donna awoke at seven without the benefit of the alarm clock. She was vaguely excited and a trifle nervous about her interview at the Incarnation Preschool, but she had no doubt that she was doing the right thing.

She showered and washed and blew her hair dry before she awakened the girls. Then for the first time in days, she applied make-up — light eye liner, blush, a touch of lavender eye shadow and pale lipstick. Not satisfied with her hair she used her curling iron"Hmm, not bad," she told her reflection approvingly. She dressed carefully in dark green panty hose, black loafers, a red and green plaid skirt, red blouse and dark green blazer. She was pleased with her image in the full length mirror on the back of her bedroom door.

Her daughters were delighted with her transformation. Mindy told her very seriously, "Mommy, you may stand outside with us to wait for the school bus." The morning routine went smoothly, and Donna did stand outside with the girls until they were safely on the bus.

After she had waved them out of sight, she picked up the morning paper and went back into the house, careful to lock the door behind her. There was no sign of the dirty pick-up truck she had seen the previous day.

She glanced at the paper over a quick cup of coffee, but found nothing of interest in it. There was still no identification of the man whose body had been found next to the cemetery. She felt sorry about the murder but reasoned that it had nothing to do with her. Anyway she had a potential new job to concentrate on.

Before she left she checked to make certain that the glass doors were locked and then she opened the door to the garage, used the automatic opener to slide the door open, shut and locked the door into the family room, backed her car out of the garage and pushed the automatic button to slide the door shut again.

She was unaware of a dirty pick-up truck following some distance behind her up the Pike Road to the church. She didn't see it slow down as she drove into the church driveway, nor did she see a man wearing a beard and a knit cap lean over and watch her as she did.

She parked in the church parking lot, and because she was a few minutes early, she sat for a few moments and watched a number of young mothers park their cars and hurry their youngsters through a side door marked, "Preschool."

The young mothers, dressed in blue jeans and sneakers, made her feel that perhaps she was overdressed.

When the flurry of activity subsided and the mothers had driven off, Donna entered the little school through the marked door. Inside she found a gold carpeted room equipped with low clothes racks and books and toys on shelves.

A sweet-faced middle-aged woman wearing navy slacks and sweater was ushering little children into an adjoining room. Donna cleared her throat and the woman turned at once and greeted her with a broad smile. She beckoned Donna to follow her.

"You must be Donna Atkins," she said. Donna nodded but before she could answer the woman continued, "I'm Marge Adams. We spoke on the phone yesterday." "I'm glad to meet you," Donna responded with a smile, but before any more could be said, another woman hurried breathlessly into the room behind them.

"This is Janet Wellborn," Marge Adams said introducing an obviously very pregnant young woman to Donna. "She's my assistant, but as you can see she'll be leaving us very soon. That's why I placed the ad which you answered."

"How do you do?" Donna and Janet said at the same time as they shook hands. "When is your baby due?" Donna asked.

"Saturday," Janet responded, "and I can't wait. I plan to work the rest of this week, though, if I can."

"Is this your first child?" Donna asked.

"Yes," Janet answered with a bright smile "It's about the most exciting thing that's ever happened to me, but I'll miss working here." She waved her arm in emphasis.

Donna looked around the room which was larger than the one through which she had entered. The floor was covered with muted brown and gold squares of vinyl upon which were standing brightly painted little tables. Surrounding the tables were equally brightly painted small straight chairs.

Decorating the wall were numerous colorful pictures of story book characters and some of Bible children. She saw that one wall was devoted to the alphabet, both upper and lower case, and also to numerals. A television set, a tiny computer and a VCR were situated against the far wall between two wide windows which afforded a clear view of a grassy lawn and a playground backed up by large evergreen trees.

The children at that moment were playing on a fuzzy blue carpet which had large colorful cushions lying about on it in a haphazard fashion. Donna counted 14 children ranging in age, she later discovered, from three to five.

Leaving Janet with the children, Marge Adams took Donna's arm and led her back into the first room and through a door on the far side which led into a small office. She sat behind the desk and offered Donna a comfortable leather chair facing her.

She went over Donna's credentials very carefully before she spoke. "You have a fine professional background," she said, "Now tell me about you."

Donna told her all about Ben and the girls and even Pal and how they were the only ones living in Brookside Farms.

"I find that especially fascinating," Marge stated, "Aren't you lonely? Does it make you nervous?"

"I must admit that it makes me feel a bit uneasy sometimes, especially when Ben is away on business. One thing that bothers me is that the girls seem to be lonely. They'd love to have nearby friends to play with. On top of that they have told me that they feel shy at school, especially Mindy.

She was surprised at herself for pouring out her feelings to Marge, a stranger, when she had never mentioned them to Ben. Marge smiled at her sympathetically. "How about spending the rest of the morning here with us?" she suggested, "You are more than welcome to stay for lunch, too. We have plenty to eat, and we'd love to get to know you better."

It was obvious to all three of them that Donna would come to work as soon as Janet went to the hospital. Donna enjoyed herself thoroughly. The children were adorable, the school was well equipped and she had developed a great rapport with both women, especially Marge.

The others watched Donna as she worked with the children, and when it was time for them to go outside to the playground Marge suggested that Donna take them. She hadn't had so much fun in ages. She played with them in the sandbox, pushed them on the swings, watched them go down the sliding board and even taught them how to skip rope.

It was almost time to take them back into the building when she thought she saw a man lurking behind the evergreen trees. Was there really a man there? Was someone watching them? Nervously she hurried the children back inside.

Marge was standing in the shade a few feet from the door when Donna herded the children out of the play yard. "Oh! Donna said, surprised. Have you been here all along?"

Marge smiled at her, "I wasn't spying on you. I was just watching you with the children. You are very good with them."

"Thanks," Donna replied uneasily. She kept looking back toward the trees, but she saw no one."Marge," she asked, "Did you see anyone in the evergreen trees?"

"In the trees?" Marge asked in surprise, "Who would that be? I didn't see anybody out here except you and the children."

"I'm so sorry," Donna said in a soft voice, "I feel like such a fool, but I could have sworn that I saw someone move back there."

"It must have been the wind," Marge laughed, "It does strange things in the woods sometimes. Or more likely it was a deer. Don't worry about it. Now lets go in for lunch."

chapter nine

t three o'clock Donna left the school for home. She was climbing into her car when Janet approached her. "It was great meeting you. You don't know how happy it makes me to know that you will be able to take my place. I mean it's so much fun working here. I know you'll love it, and Marge is an angel.

Donna laughed, "Thanks so much. I'm very happy to have the job. My husband will be thrilled, too. He's been after me to get back into preschool teaching."

Janet hesitated a moment and then spoke seriously, "Aren't you worried about those murders? I mean one was really close and the others weren't that far away. I mean, it certainly looks to me like a serial killer, don't you think so?"

"I mean you are living up in Brookside Farms all alone with just your kids until your husband gets home. You be sure to keep all of your doors and windows locked, Donna, and don't go wandering around by yourself,"

Donna laughed, "Thanks for your concern, Janet. It's so sweet of you, but why would anyone want to kill me?"

"Why would anyone want to kill the others?" Janet shot back. Donna shrugged uncomfortably. She had been thinking the same thing.

She drove into her garage at precisely 3:15, shut the door and was collecting advertisements and the phone bill from the mail box when the girls' bus arrived at 3:30.

They had both made new friends and talked all over each other in their excited desire to tell their mother all about them.

Donna was delighted, "This has been a good day all around," and she told them all about her new job.

The phone was ringing when she opened the front door. The children ran in ahead of her and down the hall to the family room and the phone. Donna hurried after them and suddenly pitched forward when Pal ran between her feet.

She saved herself from falling by grabbing the door jam at the family room entrance, but she was startled and very mad at the cat. "You've got to stop that, Pal," she shouted uselessly.

Melanie beat Mindy to the phone and grabbed the receiver, "Hello," she answered, "This is Melanie Atkins speaking."

"Hello, Melanie Atkins," said a woman's voice, "This is Hattie Farwell speaking. You have lovely phone manners. I'm kind of a neighbor, and I'm calling to welcome you and your family to the neighborhood. Is your mommy there? I'd like to speak to her."

"Thank you," said Melanie politely, "My mommy's right here. I'll get her." She turned around and yelled, "Mommy, Mommy, There's a phone call for you."

Donna laughed as she walked over to the phone, "I kinda of figured that out." Melanie handed her the instrument saying, "It's a neighbor."

"A neighbor?" Donna whispered, "I didn't think we had any." She put the phone to her ear, "Hello," She said in a louder voice,

"This is Donna Atkins." She thought, I hope it's not someone selling something.

She relaxed when she heard Hattie's sweet alto voice, "My name is Hattie Farwell, and I'm probably your closest neighbor. I live at the other end of a dirt lane which accesses your development, and I'm calling to welcome you to the neighborhood. I'd like to come meet you and your family when it's convenient for you."

"How nice," Donna responded with real pleasure in her voice, "We're not doing anything this afternoon. If you're free. I'd love to meet you."

"I'll drive right up," said Hattie.

In less than ten minutes Hattie's old but well kept Pontiac station wagon pulled up in front of Donna's house. Donna, with a little girl on either side of her, opened her front door and stepped onto the porch to greet Hattie.

She hid her surprise at Hattie's choice of clothing beneath a warm smile of welcome. Melanie, on the other hand, in her loud little girl voice piped up, "What is she wearing? Why does she dress like that?"

Continuing to force a smile Donna said through clenched teeth, "Melanie! Be quiet! Don't be rude!" Hattie, who had overheard the child, laughed. "Don't worry Melanie, many people want to know why I dress this way, and I'll tell you — I dress this way because I like to." She smiled at both children, "Does that make sense to you two?"

Mindy smiled back at her, "I think you look very nice. I like the way you dress."

Melanie realizing that Mindy had one up on her contributed, "I like the way you dress, too," And with that a bond was formed between the old lady and the little girls.

Donna felt at ease right away, "Welcome to our home," she said, "You have the distinction of being our very first guest."

"An honor," Hattie stated in her lovely alto voice, "So far everything I've seen is beautiful. I hope you'll all be very happy here." She brought a carefully wrapped loaf of bread from under her cape, "I've brought you a housewarming gift. I hope you like home baked cinnamon bread. It's fresh from the oven."

"We love it," they said in chorus. "Thank you so much. You didn't have to do that," said Donna as Hattie placed the bread in her hands, "It smells wonderful! When did you have time to bake this?"

"Well, this morning I thought that maybe you would be home today, so I made the bread then and baked it this afternoon. I tried to reach you earlier but you weren't home," Hattie admitted.

Donna helped Hattie off with her cape and hung it in the hall closet. After she and her daughters had shown Hattie around the house they all settled in the family room where Donna served everyone the bread and butter and hot chocolate.

"This is really, really fun," chirped Melanie as she bit into a slice of warm cinnamon bread, "Mmm, this bread is really, really good.'"

"Yes it is," contributed Mindy in sophisticated tones, "It is simply delicious."

"It certainly is," Donna said with a chuckle, "It's just wonderful of you to come see us. It's been a bit lonely with no neighbors. And now we have you."

"Yes," Hattie murmured. Her eyes seemed to stare into space and her face was sad.

"Are you O.K. Miss Hattie?" Donna's voice registered concern, "Did I say anything wrong?"

"What? Oh no dear," Hattie abruptly ended her reflections, "I was just reminded of my dear friend, Annie, her sad death last November and her two granddaughters. Those girls were more welcome in my house over Thanksgiving than I can express.

"They've gone back to their own lives now. Anna has married and is living in Washington State where she and her husband are teaching school. Brooke is in her senior year in a boarding school in Massachusetts. I must admit that I've been a bit lonely, too, since they've gone. And now I have you — and the children," she added with a smile, repeating Donna's statement.

"Don't you have any other neighbors?" Donna asked.

Hattie shook her head, "No, no one. We're in the country, you know," she smiled.

"Don't you ever get scared all by yourself?" Melanie burst out.

"Actually, I don't," Hattie spoke with conviction, "Anyway, I have my dog, Wolf. He's fine protection."

"Wolf?" the girls exclaimed in chorus, "Why is his name Wolf?"

Hattie explained to them very seriously about Wolf's mixed ancestry. She told them of his great size but assured them that he wouldn't bite them. As she spoke Pal jumped into her lap and purring loudly curled up and went to sleep.

Hattie stroked the cat's soft fur, "I have some cats, too," she said, "Three. Mine are really barn cats, but I feed them and they catch mice. They like it outside or in the barn better than being inside the house."

"Do they have any kittens?" Mindy asked excitedly, "I'd love to have a kitten."

"I'm sorry, dear," Hattie said, "They can't have kittens. Kittens are adorable, though, aren't they?"

Hattie lifted Pal from her lap very gently and placed him on the floor. He gazed up at her with somewhat reproachful yellow eyes. Hattie stared back at him with interest, "He looks like a little panther, doesn't he?" I believe that he's a Bombay cat."

"A Bombay cat?" said Donna, "I've never heard of that. Can you tell us anything about them?"

"As far as I know they were bred in the early 1900s by a woman who wanted them to look like miniature panthers. They all have sleek black fur and usually yellow eyes. The pads of their paws are black. Here let's see Pal's paws."

She picked up the cat and they all examined his pads. "They are black," shouted Melanie as if she had found a buried treasure. The cat growled and Hattie put him down rapidly. "That's another thing about them I understand. They can be a bit feisty."

"Well that settles it," Donna chuckled, "As beautiful as Pal is, he is feisty sometimes. If things don't go his way he has even been known to bite."

Hattie smiled, "I'll have to beware of that cat."

"Can we come see your cats soon?" asked Melanie, "I'd love to meet Wolf, too."

"And I'm sure he would like to meet you, too," Hattie laughed, "You're all very welcome to come to my house any time. But now I'd better go to my house, myself." She looked at her watch, "It's later than I thought. Wolf will be wanting his dinner, and I have a stew on the stove."

When Hattie left the house the temperature had dropped considerably and a chill wind had started to blow. She pulled her cloak tighter around her and hurried to her car. "It feels like snow," she called to the trio waving to her from the porch.

With promises of seeing each other soon and sincere thanks for the bread ringing in her ears, she drove away. No one noticed a dirty pick-up truck parked around the bend in the road.

chapter ten

attie's prediction proved true that night when a light snow began to fall. Before dawn the snow was mixed with frozen rain and the roads became treacherous. The schools were closed, much to the children's delight.

Donna was less thrilled. She was low on groceries and had planned to shop at Super King, the nearest super market, Wednesday morning. The weather changed her plans. The store was at least eight miles away, and she wasn't about to chance the drive.

The snow continued all that day and into the next night. By Thursday morning the roads were still snow and ice-covered, but a slowly rising temperature had created a heavy fog. The schools remained closed. Once again Donna decided not to go shopping.

The bearded man didn't go to Brookside Farms or anywhere else on Wednesday. Instead he stayed home in his Falls Township trailer and planned the murder of his fourth victim, a man named Joseph Townsend whom he had also been watching.

Townsend lived in Doylestown Township and worked at Super King where he was the produce manager.

The man had watched Townsend long enough to know that his routine was always the same. From 7:30 every morning when he arrived at the supermarket, Townsend was busy receiving and overseeing the arrangement of the produce. At precisely 10 o'clock, rain or shine, he left the store through a back door and smoked a cigarette in an alleyway through which the delivery trucks had come and gone.

As the bearded man had predicted, the foggy alleyway was deserted when he got there. He parked his truck in an isolated spot at the side of the building and walked into the alley.

He peered cautiously into the dense fog. Not a soul in sight.

The fog seemed thicker than ever, and he almost bumped into the two trash containers he was looking for when he saw them. One was for garbage and was emptied every day, he had discovered. The other was for cardboard and wouldn't be emptied again until Friday. As quietly as possible, he raised the double lids on that one, and pulled several layers of cardboard out of it.

He ducked behind the container a few minutes later when he heard the door to the store opening. He watched with a touch of nervousness as the large, shadowy frame of Joseph Townsend stepped into the alley.

Townsend was as tall as he was and probably outweighed him by 15 pounds.

He was also about the same age — a worthy adversary under any circumstance. He would be hard to take down unless he caught him by absolute surprise.

He had been able to knock the others out with swift karate chops to the base of their skulls, but this man was different, so to insure himself against an unexpected struggle, he had armed himself with a two-by-four ripped from a broken pallet.

A brief flare of a flame and the smell of cigarette smoke indicated that Townsend was not suspicious. The bearded man watched the periodic glow of the cigarette as Townsend drew on it, and, his adrenalin coursing, he awaited the right moment to attack.

Finally, through the haze, he saw the butt thrown to the ground and Townsend grind out the ember under his foot. He readied himself, the board in his right hand held in an iron grip.

He expected the big man to turn to go back inside the store, but he surprised him by starting toward the trash bin behind which he was crouching.

Townsend spoke aloud, obviously to himself, but the effect was unnerving, "Huh? Why are the lids open?" He took several large strides over toward the bin with the intent of closing the lids.

It was then that he spied the other man crouched there. "Who...?" Townsend started to yell, when the man leapt at him wielding the board.

Townsend, amazingly agile for his size, ducked to one side, and the board crashed down harmlessly on the edge of the bin. He lunged at his assailant, who had once again raised his club. This time a crushing blow fell on Townsend's left shoulder. With a yell of pain, he automatically grabbed for his injured shoulder with his right hand, and the board smashed into his skull.

Townsend was probably dead from the blow, his attacker thought, but he placed his huge hands around his victim's throat, anyhow, to squeeze out any life which might remain. "Goodbye, " he panted as with great effort he wrestled the large body into the trash bin, covered it with the cardboard he had removed earlier and closed the lid.

He felt buoyant as he found his way back to his dirty pickup truck. He considered himself to be a skilled killer. He loved stalking his victims, and killing them was an indescribable thrill. There was no regret because he knew they deserved to die.

"You're next, Donna," he sang in an off key baritone as he drove slowly through the swirling mist to Brookside Farms.

chapter eleven

By Thursday afternoon the fog had lifted and the girls were becoming restless. "Can we go out?" Mindy asked her mother, "I'm bored. There's nothing to do."

"Mindy, don't you have homework to do? You didn't do any yesterday. And Melanie, aren't you supposed to be reading a book?"

"Ahhh, Mommy," Mindy wailed, "That's boring, too." "Yes," agreed Melanie, "that's boring."

"You may watch television for one half hour, and then you must do your homework. There will be school tomorrow, I'm sure." Donna started for the stairs to the second floor, "I'll be vacuuming if you need me."

From her bedroom Donna heard the television click on before

she plugged in the vacuum. Then all other sounds were muted by the roar of the cleaner.

Twenty minutes later, Mindy, bored with her sister's selection of a show, stood up and walked to the sliders. The fog had cleared and one narrow shaft of sunlight illuminated the gas grill on the patio.

"Let's go out and ride our bikes," she suggested to Melanie. Melanie wrinkled her nose, "I don't know if Mommy will let us," she answered doubtfully.

"I'll ask her," Mindy volunteered and walked into the hall where she stood at the foot of the stairs. The vacuum was still roaring overhead.

"Mommy," Mindy called in a barely audible voice, "We're going out to ride our bikes." Without waiting for an answer she hurried back to her sister.

While Melanie turned off the T.V. Mindy unlocked the door to the garage. After dumping Pal back into the family room when he tried to follow them, they both stepped out, taking their coats from their pegs as they went.

Mindy pushed a button to open the outside door. They took their bikes, which were leaning against the far wall beyond Donna's car, and rode them down the driveway and up the road leaving the garage door wide open behind them.

They paid no attention to a dirty dark blue pick-up truck which drove slowly past them.

chapter twelve

bout three minutes later, Donna, who had pushed the vacuum from her bedroom into the hall, finished cleaning the hall carpet. She turned off the cleaner and returned to the master bedroom to unplug it.

There was no sound from the floor below, and Donna smiled. "Imagine," she said to herself, "they actually did what I told them to and turned off the T.V."

She pushed the vacuum to the front of the house and into the girl's bedroom over the living room. She had plugged it into the receptacle, and had started the motor when she spotted a book lying on the floor next to Mindy's bed. The book which Mindy was supposed to read at home, and on which she was to write a book report.

Obviously the child could not be doing her homework when her book was still upstairs! Mindy knew that book report was due tomorrow!

Annoyed, Donna turned off the cleaner and ran downstairs, Mindy's book in her hand.

• • •

He had seen the children ride their bikes out of the garage. When he drove past them, it was obvious they had no intention of going home soon, so he turned the truck around and parked around the bend from their house.

"That open garage door is too inviting to pass up," he thought. He was pretty certain that the little girls had not locked the door into their house, so he rapidly changed his plans about killing Donna the next day. "Today will be just fine!" he said aloud, "Door unlocked, girls out and Donna Atkins home alone! What more could I ask for?"

He stepped from his truck and walked back toward the Atkins' house. He had just rounded the bend, with the house in full sight, when Donna, coatless despite a sudden drop in temperature, rushed down the driveway from the open garage.

Although he ducked back out of sight, she was in such a panic that she didn't even look in his direction. She ran into the road, hesitated a moment, then turned and raced to the left, in the direction of the private lane.

She ran part way down two cul de sacs, but when there was no sign of Mindy and Melanie, she raced back to the road and part way around the circle until she came to Hattie's private road.

The bearded man followed her at a safe distance, ready to jump out of sight if he saw her turn toward him. When it became apparent that her search might continue for some time, he went back to his truck and parked it behind the empty house across the street from the Atkins' where it was hidden from view.

Very stealthily he moved toward the front of the house and peeked around the side. There was no sign of Donna or her children.

Cautiously he moved on toward the road. Still no one around.

He crossed the road rapidly and ran into Donna's open garage.

A quick glance around disclosed the door to the family room. Several long strides took him past Donna's car to the door. Holding his breath, he turned the knob.

To his great relief the door swung open. As he stepped across the sill, Pal pushed between his legs tripping him, and almost sending him sprawling onto the rug.

He swore under his breath and aimed a brutal kick at the cat, but Pal, too quick for him, raced into the garage and through the open door to freedom.

For a brief moment he watched the fleeing animal from the doorway. He then turned and closed the door to the family room behind him and chanced a risky but necessary survey of the house.

He started on the second floor where he discovered the master bedroom and bath in the back of the house opposite the top of the stairs. Outside the door to the bedroom he stopped beneath a trapdoor with a narrow rope hanging from it. He pulled the rope, and as he figured the trapdoor contained a descending staircase to the attic.

A chill blast of air struck him as he pulled the door open wider. With little effort he unfolded the narrow staircase and climbed up far enough to look around the attic.

Cardboard cartons, suitcases and two trunks stood near the stair opening. otherwise the attic was empty. A possible hiding place he thought, but not for long. The attic was too cold.

He climbed back down the stairs, pushed them into place and closed the trapdoor.

He stood still and listened for any sound to indicate that anyone had come into the house.

All was silent. Down a small hall past the master bedroom was a little room over the garage which had been furnished as an office.

On his immediate left in the main hall was a linen closet, and just beyond that a bathroom. To his right, extending half-way down the hall was the railing around the stairwell.

There were two bedrooms at the front of the house. The room over the living room was obviously the girls'. The one opposite, over the dining room, was furnished with an unmade queen-sized mattress in a bed frame with a small table at its side. A lamp stood on the table. An oak bureau stood against the side wall.

A guest room, no doubt, he thought. Maybe tonight I'll be the guest!

A hasty tour of the first floor revealed no potential hiding places with the possibility of the coat closet, but he didn't think that would be too great. He found the door to the basement, four inches ajar as usual, but that fact, nor the reason for it did not register with him.

He pushed the door wide open, then closed it behind him as he descended a wooden staircase into a large unfinished room in the front of the house. A furnace, oil and hot water tanks stood a few feet from the far wall, on which was fastened a circuit breaker. The only other thing in the room was a cat litter box on the floor near the stairs.

In a wall dividing the rear portion of the basement from the front were two doors. He pushed the far one open and found a well outfitted workshop. The other, to the right and rear of the stairs, stood ajar. It led to the laundry.

The cellar was warm and dry, but there was no outside entrance. That could present a problem, he thought, but judged that the windows, though high, would be large enough for him to push his bulk through in an emergency.

He decided to hide in the basement after he discovered a small lavatory containing a toilet and wash basin just off the laundry.

chapter thirteen

onna tried to think calmly as she started down the private road. Deep muddy ruts hampered her progress.

"They couldn't ride their bikes on this," she thought and was just starting to turn around when she spotted the bikes lying half hidden behind some rocks at the side of the road. There was no sign of the girls.

She hurried along as fast as she could on the slippery surface, oblivious to the chill air, but very aware that it was getting late and the sky was darkening.

"What if the murderer has gotten them? What if someone has taken them away? Are they hurt? Oh, dear Lord," she prayed, "please let them be O.K. Please, let me find them!"

On she went, sobs catching in her throat. The road twisted and turned. It seemed to have no end. She was oblivious to the cold.

"Oh, Mindy, oh Melanie, where are you?" She had never known such fear.

"What if they didn't come down this road, after all?" she thought, "Maybe they went home...No they couldn't have, I would have seen them. Where can they be?"

Her eyes swept the woods from right to left, from left to right. She was close to hysteria when she rounded a final bend in the road and saw an old farmhouse. Lights shown in its windows and a curl of wood smoke rose from its chimney.

A stepping-stone path led through a gate in a picket fence to the kitchen door. She pushed the gate open, and stopped dead in her tracks when she heard a low growl coming from the direction of the porch.

She backed through the opening and slammed the gate closed just as an enormous dog dislodged itself from the shadows and ran to her, barking furiously.

"Nice boy. Nice boy," she found herself saying in a shaky voice. The huge beast placed its front paws on the gate and looked down at her, its amber eyes appraising her. It continued its deep, loud barking, but she noticed that his tail was wagging.

She was trying to decide what to do next, when the kitchen door opened and Hattie hurried out. "WOLF!" she shouted, "OFF!" The dog immediately took its paws from the gate and moved a few feet toward Hattie. Hattie's white hair hung loosely around her shoulders, but Donna in her frightened frame of mind paid scant attention.

Wolf barked once more. "QUIET!" commanded Hattie, and the dog calmed down.

"You don't have to be afraid of Wolf, Donna," Hattie said in her deep cultured voice, "His bark is worse than his bite. Please, come in. I believe you are looking for two little girls."

"Are Mindy and Melanie here?" Donna almost shouted. Without giving another thought to the dog, she opened the gate and ran past him to the house.

Hattie smiled, and she and the dog followed quietly behind as Donna rushed into the kitchen. "I've been trying to reach you on the phone. I left a message."

"Mommy, hi!" said Melanie happily from a seat at the kitchen table. "We're drinking hot chocolate."

Mindy, sitting opposite her sister, was also drinking hot chocolate from a mug, "Hi, Mommy," she said sheepishly.

Donna hugged them both as if she would never release them. But then her relief turned to sudden anger. She stood up. "What do you mean, 'Hi, Mommy' ? You act as if nothing happened. Don't you know you scared me half to death? Why didn't you do what I told you to?

"When do you plan to do your homework? What about the book report which is due tomorrow, Mindy? WHAT-WERE-YOU-EVER-THINKING-OF-TO-SNEAK-OUT-OF-THE-HOUSE-LIKE-THAT? HOW-COULD-YOU?" Her words ran together, and she was shouting almost incoherently when she finished.

She started to shiver and began to sob uncontrollably at the same time.

Hattie led her to a chair at the table and wrapped a wool throw around her. "Here," she said pouring hot chocolate into a crockery mug, "Drink this. It will help to warm you."

She pushed a tissue into Donna's right hand, and smiled at her kindly, "Now, dry those tears. Everything is fine," she whispered soothingly.

Donna sank gratefully into the chair and sipped the chocolate. She hadn't realized how very tired she was, or how cold.

She looked around the cozy kitchen. A wood fire burning on the hearth of a walk-in fireplace, a pot of soup cooking on the stove, the aroma of bread baking in the oven and the hot chocolate gave the room a dreamy, peaceful ambience.

As she warmed up she felt herself relaxing, but she was still furious at Mindy in particular and Melanie, too. She glared at them while they drank their chocolate.

Hattie drew up a chair next to Donna's, "Welcome to my home, Donna, although I didn't anticipate such an arrival."

Donna laughed in spite of herself, "I had no business charging into your home the way I did, but they disappeared this afternoon and frightened me to death."

She looked into Hattie's clear gray eyes and saw sympathy there. "Don't even think about it, dear. You acted just like any mother would," Hattie consoled.

She hesitated for a few seconds and then asked, "There is one thing I would like to ask you since you are here. Does your husband own a dark blue pick-up truck?"

"No," answered Donna, somewhat alarmed, "Why do you ask?"

"For some mysterious reason someone has been parking it in a small clearing off my lane. When it's there it's been pretty well hidden, but Wolf spotted it a week or so ago while I was taking him for a walk. Since it wasn't too far from your road, I thought maybe you would know who owned it. I'd never seen it around until recently when it drove down my lane."

"That's strange," Donna responded, "I've seen a truck which fits that description a number of times. It's so dirty that I haven't been able to read the license plate, and the windows are filthy, too — so filthy that I can barely make out the driver except that he has a beard and seems to be wearing a knit cap." Hattie nodded, "Yes, I remember that."

At the mention of his name Wolf, who had been sleeping next to the fireplace, raised his massive head and looked adoringly at his mistress. He thumped his tail on the floor several times, yawned, and stretched out to sleep once more.

"What kind of dog is Wolf, anyway?" asked Donna, "I've never seen a dog that big in my life!"

"He's three-quarters Irish Wolf hound and one-quarter Timber Wolf," Melanie announced. Don't you remember? Aunt Hattie told us about him yesterday."

"He's really a lamb." Hattie rose as she spoke and put another log on the fire. She smiled and patted the dog's head.

"Now," she continued, "You must all stay for supper. I have fresh baked bread in the oven and homemade vegetable soup on the stove, and I would really love to have your company."

Donna demurred, but Hattie was insistent.

"Oh, please, Mommy, let's stay," begged Melanie, "It's so nice here."

"To tell you the truth, we'd love to stay," Donna said, "But I don't want to put you to any more trouble."

"Trouble indeed!" Hattie exclaimed, "You don't know how much I enjoy having company. I'm all alone here, you know, and sometimes it gets a bit lonely."

She was silent for a few moments as she ladled the rich soup into bowls. "I grew up here," she confided, "It had been my grandfather's farm and his father's before him, and then my father inherited it. It was to have gone to my brother when my parents were gone, but he was killed in the second world war.

"I was teaching school in Philadelphia, but when Fred died I came home to help my folks. I planned to go back to teaching some day, but I couldn't leave them.

"My father had a stroke shortly after the telegram arrived telling of Fred's death, and Mother was too frail to handle him by herself and still take care of the farm. So here I've been ever since, just volunteering to tutor at the girls' school when needed.

"When I became too old to take care of the farm by myself (I'll be 81 in August), I had to sell the herd and the pasture land to take care of my expenses. You'll never know how much I hated to see them go."

They ate in silence for a time, enjoying the food.

Donna was helping to clear the table and wash the dishes when Hattie suddenly put her hand to her head, "Oh my goodness! I had just washed my hair and was drying it in front of the fire when Mindy and Melanie arrived. Please, pardon me while I do something with it. I must look a fright!'"

When she was out of the room, Donna turned toward Mindy, "I am very disappointed in you," she said severely, "Have you any idea how badly you frightened me? You did a terribly sneaky thing leaving the house when I told you both to do your homework. You know that you will have to be punished, don't you?"

They both nodded soberly. In truth they had been frightened

themselves when their mother had dissolved into tears.

Hattie bustled back into the kitchen carrying her pocket book and a rust-colored sweater and wearing her black cloak. Her hair was in a tidy bun at the nape of her neck. "I'm going to drive you home," she announced in a no-nonsense voice, "Here, Donna, wear this," she ordered as she handed Donna the sweater, "It's become much too cold to go out in just that sweatshirt."

With the girls bundled into their coats and Donna in Hattie's sweater, they started toward Hattie's nine year-old Pontiac station wagon which was parked in a driveway leading to the barn. Hattie locked the kitchen door securely behind her.

"These murders have made even me a trifle nervous," she confessed, "Normally I never lock my doors." The giant dog followed silently behind them.

When Hattie opened the car's rear door, Wolf raced ahead of the girls and jumped over the back seat to curl himself contentedly in the rear of the wagon.

Hattie had just started the engine when a police car drove up the lane from the Pike Road. Jim stepped from the car and walked to Hattie's window.

"Thank you for identifying the old pick-up truck we found in the woods, Miss Hattie. Just as we suspected, with your help and the PIN number it turned out to be Mr. Tierney's."

"Thank you for telling me, Jim. I was certain that it was his car. Can you come in for a minute? I'd like you to meet my new neighbors." She turned off her engine.

Jim held Hattie's door for her, and they all trooped back into the house.

Wolf danced around Jim joyously, and Jim rubbed his great head enthusiastically.

Back inside Hattie offered Jim something to eat, but he refused saying he had just had his supper. "I wanted you to know about the old pick-up truck, and to tell you the truth I just wanted to make sure you were O.K."

"Thank you," Hattie smiled, "Your concern is most appreciated. And now let me introduce you to Donna Atkins and her two daughters Melanie and Mindy. They're the first people to live in Brookside Farms."

"Just the three of you Mrs. Atkins?" he asked.

"No," said Donna, "My husband is away on a business trip. He should be home on the weekend. And please call me Donna."

"O.K. Donna," he said, "I'll tell you the same thing I told Miss Hattie. Be sure to keep your doors locked all the time. We don't know anything about the person who has all ready killed three people in Bucks County. We don't know where he is or why he did what he did, but we are warning everybody to keep their doors locked," he repeated.

Later when Hattie drove Donna and the girls home she didn't go up her lane, "I'm taking the slightly longer way," she explained at Donna's questioning look, "I'd prefer not to get stuck in the mud!" She drove down the lane to the Pike Road.

She negotiated the 50 or so yards to the main road without trouble. "This is the way our school bus goes," piped up Melanie in a sleepy voice

"That's right, dear," said Hattie, "I see the busses going to and from school most days."

Immediately upon turning left onto the paved road they drove past a thickly wooded area, "Those are our woods, Donna," Hattie remarked, pointing to them. "but I guess you realized that."

"Um-hm," Donna mumbled in acknowledgement. She looked down at Hattie's right foot as she pressed it on the accelerator. Even encased in a high-topped black leather boot it was small and narrow — nowhere near the size of the footprint she had seen on the path the day before.

"Do you walk in there much?" she asked Hattie.

"Not too much this time of year," Hattie responded, "Why do you ask?

"Do other people?" Donna persisted without answering, "Do you know any men who might walk in the woods?"

"No, I don't," Hattie answered with a frown, "Have you seen a man in the woods?" Donna told her about the large footprint.

"I wonder where he would have come from," Hattie mused in

some concern, "As you can see, there's no parking along this road. The only access to the woods is from your development ... or... from my private lane.."

Then Donna, quietly, so as not to be overheard by the children, poured out her concerns about the dark blue pick-up truck, about the shadows she had seen, or had believed she had seen, on her patio and about the fact that she suspected she had been followed to Incarnation Preschool and the man she thought she saw in the trees there.

"With my husband away on business, and both of our families out of town, I have been feeling kind of lonely," Donna admitted, "and as I told you yesterday, it's a bit eerie living in a neighborhood without any neighbors. Perhaps I'm just being fanciful, especially with those three recent murders."

"Yes," agreed Hattie thoughtfully. They drove on in silence until they reached Donna's place. The house was well lighted inside and out, thanks to timers.

"Ohmigosh!" Donna exclaimed as she saw that the garage door was wide open and remembered that the door to the family room was unlocked. "I was so concerned about the girls that I rushed out without locking the doors!"

"Well, I'm certainly glad that I brought you home!" Hattie announced, "Wolf and I will see you safely in. C'mon, everybody."

"Look everybody," shouted Mindy, "It's beginning to snow!"

chapter fourteen

hen they all ran into the garage white snow flakes were swirling around the spotlights on the corner of the roof and leaving their damp imprints on the driveway and road.

Donna shut and locked the garage door. They hung their coats and the sweater Hattie had lent to Donna on the hooks in the garage just outside the family room door. The door, as Donna knew it would be, was unlocked.

"It might sound foolish, but I think we should send Wolf in first," said Hattie and she did just that. The big dog sniffed around, but the house remained silent, so the others followed him in.

Hattie took hold of Wolf's collar, and led the group on a tour of the entire first and second floors. When nothing appeared to be disturbed, they returned to the family room. Melanie giggled, "You know, your dog looks as big as a pony!"

It was then that Donna noticed that the basement door was closed. "How many times do I have to tell you girls to leave that door open so that Pal can get to his litter box?" she demanded.

Both girls protested that they had never closed the door, but Donna was still annoyed with them and didn't believe them.

"It's nine o'clock," Donna said somewhat tersely, "It's time for bed. Get along upstairs now. I'll be up to hear your prayers in a few minutes."

They didn't argue. "Good night, Hattie," said Mindy, "Thank you for dinner and everything." "Good night, Hattie," echoed Melanie, "Thank you."

"Her name to you is Miss Farwell," Donna corrected.

"No," said Hattie, "I told them to call me Hattie. I prefer it."

"Good night, dears," Hattie called after them. "Sleep tight."

A moment later a wail from Mindy took Donna to the bottom of the stairs. "Where is Pal?" the child cried, leaning over the railing. He's not in my bed. He's always in my bed!

"It would seem to me that maybe somebody locked him in the basement!"

Donna called up to her with little sympathy. She walked to the basement door with the intention of going down to look for the cat, but Wolf was on his haunches sniffing at the bottom of the frame.

"That cat will never come up from the cellar with the dog in the house," laughed Hattie. "Maybe Wolf and I should go home now."

"No!" Donna surprised herself with the vehemence of her response, "Please, stay. Wouldn't you like to have a cup of tea with me?"

Hattie could see that Donna was still very nervous, so she agreed to the tea, and told her she wouldn't leave until Donna was ready to part with her.

When Donna went upstairs to say good night to the children, she found Mindy in tears, and she melted. "Don't worry, honey," she soothed the sobbing child, "Pal is just afraid to leave the cellar because of Wolf. He'll be back up here in the morning."

She hugged and kissed the children. "You know I love you both more than anything else in the whole wide world," she told them. "We love you, too, Mommy," Mindy said. "We'll never scare you again," added Melanie.

Back downstairs, she put a kettle of water on the stove for tea. It was then that she suddenly remembered her answering machine and pushed the button next to the flashing red light.

Hattie's message was first, then three from Ben. No others. As if listening to his messages conjured Ben up, the phone rang.

Donna answered it on the first ring. "Where have you been?" Ben's voice was worried and accusatory. "I'm coming home on Saturday, or Friday if I can get away," he said, "This has been a nerve-wracking week away from home."

She told him about her new job at the preschool and about meeting Hattie and having dinner with her, but she did not mention the girls' disappearance or the man in the dirty pick-up truck.

She said that everything was just fine, as usual. As he always did, he told her to be careful and added, "Especially tomorrow."

"Why?" she asked curiously. "Haven't you heard?" he asked, "It's supposed to snow." "It's snowing here all ready," she responded.

As soon as she hung up she turned on the radio. She and Hattie sipped their tea and listened to the weather forecast, but only possible snow flurries were predicted. Nothing to worry about.

Having Hattie and Wolf with her was very comforting. So much so that she begged Hattie to spend the night, "We have a guest room that no one has used, yet. It would be very nice if you would stay. Please."

Hattie seeing that Donna was still upset acquiesced, "Why not?" she agreed with a smile, "Nobody is waiting for me at home."

"This may sound funny to you, Hattie," Donna said a few minutes later when she was helping Hattie to make her bed, "But I feel as though I've known you forever."

chapter fifteen

nce he had decided to stay in the basement, he felt extremely tired. He had been a trifle concerned about what would happen when Donna and the girls came home, but he knew he could handle the situation no matter what.

There was a thick red shag rug on the laundry room floor which would have to do for a bed. There was no other choice.

After he had used the toilet and washed his face and hands, he lay down on the rug. "Not too bad," he thought as he stretched comfortably, "It's strange how sleepy I get after I've killed some-one." A fading gray light was poking through the high windows when he closed his eyes and slept.

He was awakened four times by the ringing of the phone, but each time he could make out the "beep" and recorded voices of the answering machine. He could not hear what was said, however, and didn't particularly care. He simply dozed off again.

He came fully awake when he heard voices and footsteps overhead. The laundry room was pitch dark, but he hesitated to turn on the penlight which he always carried with him.

He felt his way into the front room and crouched under the stairs like a great creature of prey, every nerve alert. He heard another woman's voice talking to Donna and the children. The one thing he never expected was that they would bring someone home with them.

He was shocked that they even knew anyone to bring home. Where had he failed when he was spying on Donna all those days?

The hair stood up on the back of his neck when he heard one of the children say that the dog was as big as a pony! His alarm increased when he heard something sniffing at the door at the top of the stairs! He felt pretty certain that he knew the dog that blocked his way up into the house.

He remembered twice seeing a huge gray animal slinking silently through the woods. At first he believed it was a wolf. Especially the day that he suddenly came face to face with the beast, and it had stared at him menacingly with those startling yellow eyes.

He remembered running a few short yards to his truck, climbing in and locking the doors. The creature, which had charged right behind him, stared at him through the closed window — and barked! It might be just a dog, but it terrified him.

Now it had him trapped in the basement, unless he wanted to climb through one of those high windows, and he didn't. He'd have to find a weapon in case someone let the dog into the cellar.

Using his penlight cautiously, he crept to the door to the workshop and opened it quietly. Once in the room, he shut the door behind him and chanced turning on the overhead light.

Tools of every variety were hanging on pegboards fastened to the walls. He chose a hatchet with a well sharpened blade and stood for a long time listening.

He heard the phone ring, and vaguely made out Donna's voice. He heard the radio and the soft tones of the two women talking after Donna had replaced the phone in its cradle, but he could not hear anything they said.

The radio was turned off and finally there was the soft sound of footsteps crossing the floor, and then the house was quiet. He waited for a few more moments before he returned to the laundry and his shag rug bed. He placed the hatchet on the floor beside him.

Tomorrow, somehow, the opportunity would present itself for him to kill Donna Atkins.

chapter sixteen

attie was restless. She never slept well in a strange bed. Every little sound seemed to waken her.

She heard the door to the girls' room open and shut quietly, and she sat bolt upright. She listened carefully and was certain she heard a faint movement in the hall.

As silently as possible she stepped from her bed, and feeling her way along the wall, tiptoed to her door. She opened it a crack and listened for another sound.

There was no doubt in her mind that there was a light footfall descending the stairs. She clicked the switch by the door which turned on her bedside lamp, and strode to the table where she had left her pocketbook.

Scrambling through her purse she found a small flashlight which she always carried with her. She glanced at her watch — only 11:30. She had guessed it to be much later than that.

She did not turn off her lamp when she left her room but closed the door behind her. By using the railing of the stair-well as a guide she walked to the top of the stairs with no trouble, but at that point it was so dark that she had to turn on her flashlight.

With bare feet and clad only in one of Donna's flannel nightgowns, she went slowly down the stairs, shielding the light as much as possible. She was glad for the soft wall-to-wall carpeting and the uniform heat in the house.

Once in the downstairs hall she saw that someone had turned on the kitchen light sending a soft glow into the family room and into the hall itself. She turned off her flashlight and hurried to the back of the house in time to see the cellar door closing.

Wolf whimpered and scratched at the door. She shoved him out of the way with some difficulty, opened the door and saw that the basement light had been turned on.

The dog suddenly shoved his massive head into the opening and forced the door wide. He bounded down the steps before Hattie could stop him.

"Wolf!" exclaimed Mindy's voice from below, "I told you to stay upstairs. Maybe you like cats. Maybe you are even nice to them, but I don't think Pal would like you."

She started toward the laundry room, but the dog raced ahead of her and began sniffing at the door. His hackles rose and he emitted a deep growl.

Inside the laundry the man stood with the hatchet poised. It would be a pleasure to kill that damn dog! But what would he do about the kid? He liked kids. It would just be a damn shame to kill her, but if he must, he must.

"Move, Wolf!" commanded Mindy, "You can't come in with me!"

She forced herself between the dog and the door and reached for the knob.

"Pal," she called softly, "It's me, Pal. I'm coming in to get you. Don't be afraid."

He saw the knob turn and flattened himself against the wall so that the open door would hide him. He tightened his grip on the hatchet handle.

"Mindy, dear!" called Hattie, "Don't open that door!"

The child, startled to know anyone else was in the cellar, released the door knob and turned to face Hattie. "Why not? she demanded, and her eyes filled with tears, "I miss Pal. I can't go to sleep without him."

"I know, dear," Hattie soothed, "but you must understand that Pal will be scared to death of Wolf. He would never want to hurt you, but he might scratch you because of his great fear of the dog."

Wolf continued to sniff and snarl at the door while Mindy thought over the wisdom of Hattie's words. She stared at the giant dog and imagined what he would look like to something as small as her cat.

"I believe you are right," she stated after deep deliberation, and turned to the door, "You'll be fine in there until morning, Pal. Then I'll come and get you,"

Hand in hand Hattie and Mindy, followed reluctantly by Wolf, left the basement, turned out the lights and returned to their beds. The dog once again stationed himself at the door at the top of the basement stairs.

In the laundry the man sighed with relief. He wanted things to go his way, and this certainly had not been in his plans.

chapter seventeen

*D*onna awoke to the aroma of coffee and bacon. Her thinking was still fuzzy after a night of deep and much-needed sleep, and for a few moments she thought Ben was home and cooking breakfast.

When she became fully awake, she realized it was only Friday, and Ben was still in Pittsburgh. She frowned and looked at her clock.

"Heavens!" she said aloud, "It's almost eight!" Then she remembered the strange events of the previous day and her guest, Hattie.

She threw on her robe and ran down to the kitchen where she found Hattie at the stove and the girls sitting at the counter happily devouring pancakes and bacon. The enormous Wolf was sitting on the floor between their stools, drooling.

Hattie was wearing her long black skirt and white blouse, and the girls were dressed for school. "Good morning, Mommy," they said in unison.

"Good morning, Donna," Hattie said cheerfully, "We thought we'd let you sleep a little longer. Did you have a good rest? Would you like a cup of coffee?"

"Yes, I'd love a cup of coffee, please," Donna answered, "and good morning to all of you. Thanks for letting me sleep in a bit. I really needed it. I had a very good rest." She took the mug of coffee which Hattie handed her and added, "Thank you, Hattie. You shouldn't be doing all of this work."

She started for the stove, but Hattie pushed her to a stool at the counter and placed a plate containing three rashers of bacon and four pancakes in front of her. Helping herself to the same she sat next to her, "I'm having the time of my life, Donna. I hope you don't mind."

"Mind? said Donna, "You're like an angel from Heaven. You can't begin to know how much I appreciate everything you've done for us." She passed butter and syrup to Hattie and then helped herself. "Oh, this is wonderful!" she exclaimed between mouthfuls.

Neither Hattie nor Mindy mentioned Mindy's trip to the basement in the middle of the night.

No one had bothered to open the drapes over the glass sliders, but when Donna carried their breakfast dishes to the dishwasher, she saw snowflakes falling outside the window over the sink. "It's still snowing," she said in surprise.

"Didn't the weather person last night say we were just having snow flurries?" asked Hattie in amusement, "Let's see what the forecast is for today."

Donna turned on the television and in a few minutes the weather came on. Scattered snow showers were predicted with little accumulation. She returned to the window, "the lawn is completely covered," she said doubtfully.

The phone rang as she spoke. When she picked up the receiver she heard the sweet voice of Marge Adams, "Donna?" Donna replied in the affirmative. "Good morning, Donna," Marge greeted her, "I hope this notice isn't too late, but we'll be needing you at Incarnation from now on. Janet went into labor during the night, and her husband just drove her to the hospital. I hope you can come in today."

"Why yes, of course I can be there. Just give me a chance to dress and I'll be there as soon as I get the girls off to school."

Donna turned to Hattie, "The girls' bus doesn't get here until 8:30. Would you mind waiting until I take a quick shower? Then I have to go to work. That was Marge Adams, my new boss. She told me that the woman I am to replace has just been taken to the hospital. She's having a baby. I get out at 3:00 but I really have to get to the supermarket if we want to eat again," she added with a laugh.

Hattie laughed too, "Don't worry, Donna," she said, "If you approve, the girls can get off their bus at the end of my lane and come to my house after school. That way you won't have to worry about them when you go shopping. I'll call the school."

"Oh, Hattie, how did I ever get along without you?" Donna sighed. She turned and ran upstairs to shower and dress.

"I forgot to ask Mommy when we are going to get our bikes," Mindy remarked after her mother had left the room, "I guess we'll have to wait 'till after school. Frankly, it's not a subject I want to bring up again for awhile."

Hattie roared with laughter, "I believe you are correct, dear. I think after school would be fine."

Donna, wearing navy slacks and a red sweater, ran back into the family room in 10 minutes. How's that for speed?" she demanded and responded to their applause with a deep bow.

She noticed that the drapes were still drawn over the sliders as she was pulling her boots on. She decided to open them later. She took her shopping list from a drawer at the side of the counter, "Can I get you anything at the store, Hattie? Or would you like to go with me?"

"No, thank you, dear. As much as I enjoy your company, I don't need anything at the store right now." She strode toward the door to the garage for her coat and sweater. Donna and the girls followed her, but no amount of coaxing could get Wolf away from the cellar door. Finally Hattie had to go back for him. She was forced to grab his collar and almost drag him into the garage.

Donna locked the house door behind them. When she raised the outside door they were all surprised to see that it was snowing steadily.

chapter eighteen

attie with Wolf in the rear of her station wagon drove off just as the school bus stopped in front of the house. Donna waved goodbye to Hattie and then to the girls. She scooped the morning paper in its plastic wrap from the snow in the driveway climbed into her car and threw the paper into the passenger seat. After she backed into the driveway she used the remote control to shut the garage door.

"Some flurry," she grumbled as she drove up the pike toward the preschool. The road was snow-covered all ready, and she was afraid of skidding, "I've never seen such weather!"

With some difficulty she maneuvered her car up the steep driveway to the preschool and found there was only one other car in the lot. Marge Adams met her at the door, "I don't think we'll have school today," she said. "The mothers have been calling ever since I talked to you. They just don't want to chance driving their children in this weather. I'm sorry I wasn't able to reach you. I did try, and I left you a message."

"That's O.K.," Donna was relieved, "I have to go to the store anyway, and I'm not anxious to be out too long, myself." She smiled at Marge as they agreed that Donna would start work on Monday. "Is there any news about Janet?"

"Not yet, but I'll let you know as soon as I hear anything." Marge put on her coat and followed Donna outside, locking the door behind her, "Ooh, this weather is terrible. Do drive carefully, Donna."

"Believe me, I will, and you drive carefully, too." They both climbed into their cars, and with Donna leading the way they made their ways slowly down the drive to the Pike Road.

Donna, wondering if she was making a mistake, turned right in the direction of the supermarket and waved goodbye to Marge who turned in the opposite direction toward her home. She watched through her rearview mirror as Marge's red taillights rapidly disappeared in the whirling snow. She still wondered if she was foolish not to go home herself.

She turned on her car radio. A commercial was airing soon followed by the weather report. "A revised weather report," the announcer's voice explained, "This is a storm advisory from the National Weather Service. We are expecting a full blown blizzard. The storm which was predicted to blow itself out in Ohio and Western Pennsylvania has picked up additional strength and is now approaching Eastern Pennsylvania, New Jersey and New York. A storm warning is in effect for those areas.

"Emergency coordinators are ordering all parked cars to be removed from emergency routes. The roads are rapidly filling with drifts and are treacherous. Drivers are requested to stay off the roads except where absolutely necessary."

"GREAT!" Donna shouted in some fear, "I don't need that!" Fat snowflakes were blowing against her car and piling up on her windshield faster than the wipers could clean them off.

She realized that she had reached the supermarket. When she started to turn into the parking lot her car skidded and spun halfway around. Her heart was beating so fast that it took her breath away. She could barely see through the snow but decided that since she was there she would simply buy milk, bread and eggs and hurry on home.

As she pulled farther into the lot of the shopping center she was surprised to see yellow crime scene tape strung across the front of the supermarket. Two police cars with flashing lights were parked by the doors, and officers and store employees were milling around next to the building.

Maybe there was a robbery she theorized as she pulled over to park. She had no idea how close she was to an actual parking space, but there were not enough cars around to make a difference.

A small curious crowd was forming near the tape, so she left her car to join them and see if she could find anyone to give her some information. As she approached, an ambulance pulled slowly from the rear of the building and left the parking lot, its headlights piercing the falling snow. It was followed by a third police car. "What happened?" she asked a man standing near her.

"A body was found in a dumpster in the alley, I heard," he answered, "That's all I know."

A police officer approached the crowd, "Sorry folks but you'll have to move along now. The store's closed."

Mingled questions of "What happened?" and "Whose body was found in the dumpster?" "Was it a man or a woman?" "Was the person murdered?" "When did the person die?" "How?" "Did the dead person work in the supermarket?" were ignored by the police officer. He simply herded them away from the store.

Donna turned around and walked slowly back to her car. She looked for a familiar face hoping someone could tell her what had happened. Her feet were cold and wet where snow had invaded her boots, and she was relieved to get into the dry car.

While she sat trying to decide what to do next she unfolded the newspaper and gasped when she saw a photograph of Tanya Williams at the top of the front page. The headline read:

MURDERED WOMAN IDENTIFIED

"Oh, no!" she cried, "Oh, no, not Tanya!" She wept as she read the story of Tanya's death. It was just awful knowing that a woman she knew had been murdered. It was too horrifying.

She peered through her snow covered windshield and recognized a check-out clerk standing away from the others. She was puffing nervously on a cigarette. Every once and awhile she wiped tears from her eyes.

Donna rolled down her window. "Excuse me," she called to the clerk. The woman looked over at her and seemed to recognize her. Even through the snow Donna noticed that the clerk was pale and shaken, "Can you tell me what happened?" she asked.

"I'm sorry," the clerk answered in a hoarse voice, "The police told us not to say anything."

"Oh please!" she begged as she stepped out of her car and approached the woman, "Is it true that someone was murdered? Please tell me. It's very important to me. Was it someone who worked here?"

"Yes, he worked here," the woman almost whispered. His name was Joe.

"I don't know his last name. He went out for his usual cigarette at around 10 o'clock yesterday morning. I saw him go.

"We were very busy, and no one thought much about him for a long time. Later we realized that he was nowhere around. We just thought that he had gotten sick and gone home. He had worked here for more than 30 years and he had a wonderful record, so when he didn't show up this morning we knew that something was wrong. The manager tried to reach him on the phone, but his wife said he had never come home last night. She said she was worried to death about him. She was afraid he had been in an accident. She called the hospital and the police, but they knew nothing about him.

"This morning the trash hauler was dumping cardboard from the dumpster when he saw part of an arm and a hand. He came inside in a panic and the manager called the police."

"How was he killed?" Donna stammered, sure that he had been strangled.

"Nobody has said," the clerk told her, "I guess they'll have to wait until the autopsy."

"Was he the produce manager?" Donna asked, "A big man with a nice smile?"

"Yes, that was Joe — nice to everyone. He always had a smile on his face. Please," the woman whispered, "Please don't tell anyone I told you this."

Donna was nearly paralyzed with fear. She was almost certain now that she knew the identity of the killer and why he was murdering specific people such as Tanya and Joe. She was convinced that she had made the connection between the victims and that she was on the killer's list.

The old man in St. Matthews churchyard, Tierney was the name Jim used. Ohmigosh, it was Timothy Tierney — Tim! She wracked her brain trying to think through her panic. And what about Marla Coulton? Marla?—Marla?—Marla? A distant bell rang in her head. I should know who Marla was. I can't think. She wanted to scream.

She stood in the swirling snow. The flakes were smaller now and coming down harder than ever, but Donna scarcely noticed. Snowflakes froze on her eyelashes and stung her face while she tried to control herself.

chapter nineteen

attie, with Wolf pacing about in the back of her station wagon, was a bit unnerved as she steered carefully down her lane to her house.

The dog had never acted like this before. What was the matter with him? Maybe it was just the snow.

She parked with care next to the barn and fought her way to the house through the wind and drifting snow. Wolf didn't want to go with her. How unusual. "What is the matter with you, Wolf? Now you come into this house at once!" she commanded.

He obeyed slowly with his head and tail hanging in protest. Hattie, grateful to be inside, hung her wet cape on a hook next to the door. With a large terry cloth towel she proceeded to wipe the snow from the dog's thick fur.

She started a fire in the fireplace, put a kettle on for tea and sat in her rocking chair by the hearth to think.

She frowned deeply trying to delve into the question of Donna's dilemma. There was no doubt in her mind that the young woman was in trouble, but why? Who was the man who was following her — spying on her? What harm did he plan to do to her? Why?

Where was the killer now in this terrible blizzard? Was he in his home wherever that was? A logical, more frightening thought grew in Hattie's mind. The killer was in Donna's laundry!

He had been there since yesterday! She never thought that someone was in the basement, but she should have suspected it. She remembered Donna scolding her daughters for closing the cellar door and the girls denying it. Of course! Donna made it clear that the door was always left open a few inches to allow Pal, the cat, to get down to his litter box.

How dumb I was, she thought. I knew that a man was following Donna. I knew that her house had been left unlocked and the garage door open for several hours. We searched the first and second floors, but why didn't we go into the basement?

Clearly because Wolf was sniffing at the door and we believed he was after the cat. Preposterous! Wolf never bothers cats. He was aware of the stranger.

And later that night when Mindy went looking for Pal no wonder Wolf growled at the door to the laundry room. He would never have acted that way if it had been only a cat.

She grabbed up the phone and dialed Incarnation Preschool hoping against hope that Donna was there, but there was no answer. She then called Donna's number. As she knew she would she got the answering machine.

"Donna," she recorded trying to sound as normal as possible in case the killer could hear her, "I called the school and the girls' bus will drop them here any minute. I'll bake a cake and we can have a snow party. You are more than welcome to attend, so hurry on over here as fast as you can."

She knew that was very weak, but she didn't know how to warn Donna without alarming the killer. Would she come? She just had to get out of that house! But how could she drive in this weather? Where was she now?

Then she phoned police headquarters, but all of the officers were out. She left a message for Jim Sawyer to call her as soon as possible. Please hurry, she thought.

Unable not to do anything, she decided to call the district attorney's office. "Please be there," she whispered as his phone rang several times.

chapter twenty

*C*rouched beneath the cellar stairs Mahlon Everly had heard Donna with the other woman and the little girls leave the house that morning. He thought the giant dog had gone out with them, but he didn't want to chance going upstairs until he was absolutely certain.

He knew he had time to wait, because he had heard Donna's discussion about going to the preschool and then the supermarket. He figured she had at least a 15 or 20 minute drive each way in good weather, and judging by the snow piling up against the cellar windows, probably a much longer trip than that.

Even if school closed early, she would still spend an hour or so shopping, so he didn't expect her home until early afternoon at the soonest.

The phone rang twice while he waited, but he was unable to hear the messages.

He crept up the stairs and listened for the dog. There was no sound. He knocked gently on the door. Still no sound. The dog was definitely not there.

He opened the door and walked into the kitchen where he found coffee, still hot, in the coffee maker. He helped himself to a cup, turned on the television and sat in a chair in the family room to watch it.

The news was full of blizzard stories but there was nothing about the murder of Joe Townsend. He was disappointed but guessed it was too soon. However there were pictures of Tanya Williams — one when she was beauty queen in high school and one taken when she was older with her mother and father at their house in Tampa, Florida.

"Is there a serial killer on the loose?" asked the commentator.

"No!" Mahlon Everly answered him, "These people sent me to prison! They have to pay for that."

He emptied the coffee pot, and while he stood at the counter the phone rang shrilly and startled him. The phone and the answering machine sat on the counter next to where he was standing. He listened to Ben's recorded voice saying, "Hi, this is Ben and Donna. We can't come to the phone right now, but if you will leave a message at the sound of the beep we'll get back to you as soon as possible." Then he listened as Hattie told Donna that she and the girls would have a snow party when they came home, and they wanted Donna to attend. She also said that she had called the school and the bus would bring them to her lane.

"I'm glad the kids are O.K. Everly said, but I'm sorry lady, Donna won't be going to your snow party or anywhere else ever again." He smirked maleficently at the answering machine.

He walked to the other side of the counter where he made himself two slices of toast, spread them with margarine and grape jelly, and ate them with a second cup of coffee while he watched the snow swirl down outside the windows over the sink.

The phone rang again. A Marge Adams told Donna that Anne Wellborn had a baby daughter and they were both doing well.

"Enough of this damn nonsense," he growled. He took a sharp kitchen knife from a rack and went out through the garage to cut the phone wires. The snow was falling so rapidly that his footprints were obliterated almost immediately.

That done he plotted where he would wait for Donna. He decided it would be a mistake for him to return to the cellar. No, this time he would go upstairs. He would wait in the girls' bedroom where he could watch through the window for her car.

He had decided on the perfect place to wait for her in ambush.

In the meantime District Attorney Ralph Allen and the county detectives scratched their combined heads, figuratively speaking, and strove to discover the identity of the serial killer.

"What was his motive?" asked the D.A.

"The method of the killings is the same indicating one killer. He strangled them all.

"The only crime scene evidence turned up was a two by four taken from a skid behind the supermarket where Joe Townsend's body was found. No fingerprints.

"The connection with the victims, after careful detective work, turned out to be Mahlon Everly's trial 12 years ago for the strangling death of his wife. The obvious connection between the victims is that they were all on the jury."

chapter twenty-one

*I*n his fourth floor office in the Bucks County Courthouse District Attorney Allen looked across his desk and down the conference table which was placed at right angles to his desk. Chief Deputy District Attorney Carolyn Parkins sat in the first seat on his right. The three other chairs closest to the desk were taken by county detectives.

"The pattern of these murders is obvious now," said Allen soberly. "The first victim was identified as Timothy Tierney by a Bristol florist and friend, Angela Fiori. He was retired, a widower and had no relatives. His dental work confirmed his identification.

Twelve years ago Tierney was the foreman of the jury which found Mahlon Everly guilty of third degree murder in the strangulation death of his wife. The district attorney spoke slowly and deliberately. The meeting was being recorded.

He stared morosely through the window at the falling snow and continued, "The second victim was Marla Coulton who was Marla Bracken at the time of the trial. Number three was Tanya Williams. Obviously Everly planned the killings in the order of the jurors' numbers

Number four was Joseph Townsend, produce manager at Super King, whose body was found this morning in a dumpster behind the supermarket. All of these people were strangled to death as was Everly's wife 13 years ago.

Now, it is of the utmost importance that we find and protect juror number 5. Her name was Donna Blake at the time — Donna Atkins now, and I don't know where she lives.

It wasn't until Tanya Williams' body was identified that we realized the connection between the victims and began our search for the remaining members of Everly's jury. We learned yesterday that about two weeks ago Mrs. Atkins and her husband and two little girls moved away from their rented home in Middletown, but as yet we haven't learned their new address.

The district attorney was interrupted by the ringing of phone. He stared at the instrument a moment as if wondering if someone else would answer it. Then he realized that his office staff had left early because of the storm, and he briefly considered not answering it at all. However he did lift the receiver.

"District Attorney Allen," he answered briskly in a hurry-up-and-get-it-over-with kind of tone.

"I'm sorry to bother you, Mr. Allen," Hattie said on the other end of the line after she had identified herself, "but I'm deeply concerned about a neighbor of mine in the Brookside Farms development. I believe that she's in terrible danger."

The district attorney knew of Hattie's work with the police in uncovering the killer of two women last November, and he had great respect for her. "Please go on Miss Farwell," he said with interest.

"Her name is Donna Atkins, and..."

Allen interrupted her, "You must be a mind reader. We have

been looking for her. Do you know where she is?"

"She lives at 57 Running Brook Circle in Brookside Farms. That's in Plumstead Township. It's the only house that's occupied in the entire development. It's new, you know. I' m very much afraid that the serial killer is hiding in her house.

Her husband is away on business, and her children are coming to me, thank goodness, but Donna is all alone. She is in grave danger, I know. The man has been following her, spying on her ever since they moved in almost two weeks ago."

She proceeded to describe the way Donna left the garage door open and the house door unlocked the day before. She told him about Wolf's behavior and her conviction that the man had been hiding overnight in the laundry.

"We'll get someone out there as soon as we can," said Allen, "I'm afraid that phoning her would be a mistake, wouldn't it?"

Hattie told him about her call and agreed that his phoning might really create more of a problem than already existed. "I might try again myself, though. I feel so helpless."

"Miss Farwell, under no circumstances are you to go over there. You would only be putting your own life in jeopardy."

"I can't get out anyway," Hattie answered, "I'm snowed in and I just don't know what to do."

"Thank you so much for calling, Miss Farwell. You have been a great help. I'll do everything in my power to get to Mrs. Atkins." and he hung up wondering what in the world he could do.

The district attorney looked at the other four who nodded their heads when he said,. "I guess you know what that call was about. I'll call the Plumstead Township Police and see if someone can be sent out to 57 Running Brook Circle as soon as possible.

"I want to thank all of you for the fine job each of you has done in uncovering information so rapidly. Now, thanks to Hattie Farwell we know where Donna Atkins is, but I have great fear that Everly is hiding in her house. I can only pray that we get to her in time."

The district attorney, conscious again of being recorded, continued with the history of the case, "As you discovered, Mahlon

Everly was released from Rockview State Prison on February 18. As you know, 12 years ago the jury found him guilty of third degree murder but mentally ill.

"Judge Manfred T. Logan sentenced Everly to 10 to 20 years in Norristown State Mental Hospital. However three years ago psychiatrists declared him mentally competent and he was transferred to Rockville State Prison.

"He could have been released two years ago, but he attacked a guard. Even though he was made to serve another two years, he's out now in spite of everything." The D.A.'s tone was bitter.

"Everly, who defended himself at his trial, threatened not only the jury but Judge Logan and you, Carolyn," The district attorney looked at her and continued for the benefit of the recording, "Carolyn Parkins was the prosecuting attorney."

He turned to Parkins, "We will give you round the clock protection until Everly is found, "Of course we will also protect Judge Logan and the other jurors. As soon as Atkins is safe and the rest of Everly's intended victims are under protection, I will talk to the press. Reporters have been calling since the first body was found.

"Above all it is essential that we do not alert Everly that we are on to him."

One of the detectives, a middle-aged man named Tom Bradley, spoke up, "We have further information on Everly. As you know he is on parole for the remainder of his sentence. Eight more years. He reported to his parole officer once since he was released from prison and has failed to show up since."

chapter twenty-two

Back in her car again Donna put her head down against the steering wheel and sobbed. She knew who the killer was. "Mahlon Everly," she said aloud in a small voice, "Mahlon Everly is the murderer!"

She remembered 12 years ago sitting in the jury box next to Joe Townsend. She clearly remembered Tanya Williams, too. She was a fun loving woman in her late 30s. She was older than Donna but didn't act it. She sat next to Joe in the third seat. Next to her sat Marla in the second seat. Marla Bracken she was then. The paper said she had just been married. That's why she had been confused by the name Marla Coulton.

The first one murdered was Timothy Tierney, the jury foreman. What a dear little man. How awful the whole thing was right from the beginning. Now the first four jurors have been murdered and I am number 5! She was terrified at the knowledge.

She remembered distinctly the awful fear that the defendant, Mahlon Everly, had instilled in all of the jurors. A huge angry man whom they had found guilty of strangling his wife.

"I'll get you," he had screamed at the jurors as the sheriffs deputies handcuffed him and led him struggling from the courtroom. Then he had turned his wrath on Judge Manfred T. Logan and on the prosecuting attorney, Assistant District Attorney Carolyn Parkins. "I'll get all of you!" he screamed, "You can count on that!"

Most of all she remembered his eyes — the palest she had ever seen. So pale that they looked as though he had no irises.

"Oh, dear Lord," she prayed aloud, "What'll I do now? That old pick-up truck with the bearded man inside. Was that Mahlon Everly? Oh, dear Lord, it had to be. He was stalking me. Planning to kill me." she sat frozen in fear, unable to concentrate. Unable to move.

"I have got to get hold of myself. I have got to get hold of myself. I have got to get hold of myself," Donna recited like a mantra.

"Oh, what'll I do now? Thank heaven the girls will be with Hattie, but I want to go home. Look at that snow! Maybe I'd better tell the police first." she looked desperately around, but there was not a policeman in sight, "I'll call Jim Sawyer from home, that's what I'll do, and I'll call Hattie, too."

She drove very slowly from the parking lot, found her way onto the road and made her careful way home. Several times she skidded, once she nearly crashed into another car which was stuck in the middle of the road, and finally she almost missed her turn into Brookside Farms. The wind whipped the snow into great drifts.

It took her three tries to get into her own driveway and around to face her garage. She pressed the button to raise the door, but nothing happened. Realizing that it was pretty well snowed shut, she took a shovel from her trunk and carefully shoveled the snow away from the door. Finally, to her relief, it opened.

She drove her car through the open door into the garage and made certain that the door closed firmly behind her. She unlocked the door into the house, hung her soaking wet coat on the hook by the door, removed her equally wet boots and socks, locked the door behind her and with a sigh of relief went into her house.

Upstairs in the girls' bedroom, Everly saw Donna's car coming up the driveway. When he heard the garage door slide closed he set his plan into motion and left the room.

It's so good to be safe at home at last, she thought as she started a fire in the family room fireplace then went into the kitchen to pour herself a cup of coffee. However the coffee maker was empty. "That's funny," she said aloud, "I was sure it had a couple of cups left in it. I guess I'm going nuts." She measured out more coffee and water.

She checked her answering machine and found two calls waiting. One was from Hattie telling her that she had contacted the school and the girls were going to her house. She said something silly about having a snow party and wanting Donna to attend. She would call her back and decline.

The other was from Marge. Anne had a seven pound six ounce daughter. They were both doing fine. As soon as the weather permits I'll buy her a present and go to see her, Donna thought.

The drapes were still closed across the sliding glass doors to the patio, so while the fresh coffee brewed Donna walked over and pulled the cords to open them. They had barely parted when she saw a pitiful sight outside.

Pressed as close to the doors as possible, half buried in snow and soaking wet was Pal! He was on his hind legs scratching weakly at the doors. His meow was silent through the glass, but Donna saw his mouth form the plaintive sound.

In one hard jerk she pulled the drapes wider open and unlocked the glass doors. She slid them apart as fast as possible with the result that a pile of heavy snow collapsed into the room with the almost limp cat.

With some difficulty she managed to push the snow away and slide the doors closed again and lock them. She wrapped Pal in some terry cloth dish towels and gently dried his dripping fur before the fire.

The little animal responded well to the warmth and loving care he was receiving and soon wriggled free of Donna's arms to go look into his food dish.

Donna opened a can of Salmon Supreme cat food and emptied it into the little bowl. Pal, who usually ate less than half that much, devoured his meal and jumped into the recliner to curl up near the fire for his nap.

Donna picked up the phone to return Hattie's call but found the line dead. "Darn blizzard," she exclaimed.

chapter twenty-three

Donna felt like a dishrag. She decided that as long as the girls would be with Hattie, she would go upstairs, take a bath and go to bed for a nap. After that she hoped she would feel better and be able to think more clearly.

She opened the door to the basement the usual four inches for Pal's convenience and, carrying a cup of hot coffee, dragged herself toward the stairs to the second floor. Something very important was nagging at her, but she was too tired to worry about it now.

Since the master bathroom contained only a stall shower and no tub, and she felt in need of a deep, hot bubble bath, she headed to the main bathroom which the girls used. When she was at the top of the stairs and turning toward the main bathroom, a blast of cold air struck her face.

She looked up and saw that the trapdoor to the attic was open a few inches. She stopped with the idea of closing it when she saw a face looking back down at her!

She screamed and for a moment was frozen in place.

As if in slow motion, the door opened wider and an enormous man came crashing down toward her, his white eyes glaring at her, his yellow teeth exposed in a vicious snarl. MAHLON EVERLY!

She screamed again, even louder. And then her adrenaline began to course through her body.

As the huge man grabbed at her, she threw her scalding coffee in his face and turned and ran to the top of the stairs.

Behind her she heard him yowl in pain and begin to curse. She was three steps down the stairs when he reached over the railing and clamped his huge hand over her left arm. Donna screamed again and tried to pull away from him.

He was hurting her so badly that she feared he would break her arm. His face, already turning red and sore from the burning coffee, was right in front of hers — a frightening and evil face. Despite the pain of the burn, he laughed!

Terrified, she screamed again, and clawed at his injured cheek with the fingernails of her right hand.

He gasped in pain, and for the briefest moment released his grip on her arm. As she pulled away and started on down the stairs he seized the arm of her sweater and hauled at it, all the time snarling like a beast and uttering a string of vile profanities.

Again a scream came unbidden from her throat. As she yanked her arm away, her sleeve tore loose in his grasp. and his fingernails raked her shoulder.

On the other side of the woods Wolf was more agitated than Hattie had ever seen him. He continuously pranced from her to the door whining and crying to get out.

He paced back and forth whimpering relentlessly until she finally had the knob turned and both the inside and storm doors opened. Once free Wolf bounded across the snow-laden porch and into a deep snow drift which completely covered the steps.

The wind continued to hurl icy snow flakes at the house, the road and the barn.

The dog leapt up over the drifts. He seemed to attack the snow as he ran across the road and into the woods, hurling his great body forward into the snow and then leaping above it.

He seemed to be driven by a voice Hattie couldn't hear. "It must be the storm," she said shrugging her shoulders in perplexity.

She closed the door and stepped to the phone to try once again to reach Donna, but her line was dead. She tried the number once more to no avail. She was thinking of calling the phone company when she heard stomping feet on her kitchen porch.

Mindy and Melanie came rushing through the door laughing. Their eyes were bright and their cheeks pink. "Hi!" they greeted Hattie. "Hi, Miss Hattie! Isn't the snow wonderful?"

In the meantime their terrified mother didn't think so. She raced to the bottom of the stairs and through the dining room into the kitchen end of the family room.

The wind howled outside and icy snowflakes banged against the windows like handfuls of pebbles. She knew it would be impossible to escape him outside in the deep snow, but where could she go? What should she do?

She took deep breaths in an effort to keep calm. Above all she had to keep her wits about her. She heard his heavy footsteps thumping down the stairs and along the hall.

Her heart raced so fast that she could scarcely breathe.

Suddenly she saw Wolf outside the sliding glass doors. He was leaping at the doors barking and scratching at them with his front paws.

Everly was coming down the hall. She couldn't get to Wolf. She saw him throw back his head and howl. A loud eerie sound starting low in his throat and ascending several octaves. A chilling throwback to his wild ancestors.

There was no time for her to run across the room, unlock the three locks and slide the doors open for Wolf. Everly was almost on top of her. She ran back toward the dining room.

When she passed the door to the basement steps she gave it a mighty push, swinging it wide open. "Oh, Lord," she prayed, "Please make him think I've gone down cellar."

The sound of Pal scratching in his litter box drifted up to her when she pushed the cellar door open. It's funny how such noises register even in panic, she thought. And at that moment, too late, she remembered what had been nagging at her.

If Pal was outside, who or what was in the basement all night? Who let Pal out? — Mahlon Everly! Of course. Of course. Even the fact that the cellar door was closed should have been a clue. If only I had realized that. That and Wolf's behavior.

She ran into the dining room as fast as she could and ducked under the old oak table trying to hide behind the center pedestal. She heard Everly charging toward the cellar stairs.

Would he run past them? If he came into the dining room he would no doubt find her. Where could she hide? Should she run back into the center hall and continue this mad chase around and around until he caught her or she collapsed with exhaustion?

Wolf howled again.

If I sneak down to the back of the hall, I'll know whether he goes down cellar or around to the back of this room. If I race to the sliding doors, I might be able to let Wolf in before Everly knows where I am, she thought desperately. And she tip-toed rapidly down the hall.

She heard his footsteps starting down the cellar stairs and waited until she figured he had reached the bottom. In a great rush she started for the sliding doors to admit Wolf, but before she was a quarter of the way across the family room she heard a maniacal laugh behind her.

She whirled around to see the huge man coming back up the cellar stairs.

"Did you really think you could fool me so easily?" he demanded as he climbed up another step. He was half-way up now. Blood oozed from the scratches on his burned cheek. His white eyes were wide.

She judged the distance to the doors and realized she could not get there and unlock them before he reached her. But what else could she do but try?

Wolf howled again, and she continued to run toward him.

Everly was laughing his frightening laugh. He was obviously having a great time playing cat and mouse with her. He could get to her in a couple of swift strides, and they both knew it.

Donna could tell by the sound of Everly's steps that he was nearing the top of the stairs. He was having fun tormenting her, coming up one-by-one, one-by-one.

She had reached the doors and had begun to fumble with the locks at the handles when she heard a loud roar from Everly, "NO YOU DON'T!" and he started to charge up the three remaining steps. He was laughing at her!

Donna's hands were shaking so badly that she couldn't turn the locks. She felt as though her whole body had turned to mush. The great dog looked through the glass at her expectantly, but she couldn't help him.

But Everly didn't rush across the floor and grab her. Instead there was a loud crashing and thumping as the gigantic man tumbled backward down the stairs and struck his head on the concrete basement floor where he lay motionless.

He had been on the next to top step when he heard a noise behind him. He was turning to see what caused it when Pal ran between his legs and tripped him.

Donna stared shocked and speechless watching Pal run through the cellar door and down the hall. "Pal tripped him," Donna gasped

She hurried to the top of the stairs and looked down at Everly's prostrate form. "Pal ran between his legs and tripped him when he was on the stairs!" she murmured, and she burst into tears, "Pal saved my life."

Leaving the cellar door open, but fearing that Everly might regain consciousness at any moment, Donna recrossed the room and quickly opened the patio doors to let Wolf into the house. Drifts fell onto the floor, and wind-driven snow blew into the room.

chapter twenty-four

hile the girls drank hot chocolate and ate fresh baked vanilla cake with chocolate icing, Hattie walked rapidly across the kitchen floor to the door. Wolf had been gone a long time, and she was getting worried about him out there in the storm.

She turned the latch and the frigid wind blew the door open with such force that she was pushed backward a few feet. The storm door was slamming back and forth. Apparently the girls hadn't latched it when they came in.

With great effort she reached out and pulled the storm door shut. She looked through its window at the mounting snow. Despite the fact that the porch was covered by a wide roof, the snow was several feet deep on its floor.

Hattie strained to see if Wolf was nearby, but she could see nothing but small, white swirling flakes. She called his name several times as loudly as she could, but her words were thrown back at her.

She turned to shut the inside door and go back to the girls when she heard Wolf's howl. Chills ran up her spine.

The only other time she had heard him emit that loud eerie sound was two years ago when she fell over a rake handle in the garden. Her breath had been knocked out of her body, and for a brief spell she was unable to get up.

Wolf was only 8 months-old at the time and very worried about her. He sniffed around her desperately, and when she didn't get up he sat back on his haunches, threw his chin up and howled.

Hattie had no doubt that the howl was coming from the Atkins' house and that Donna was in grave trouble.

She shoved the door shut against the wind and turned and hurried out of the kitchen.

"I'll be right back," she told the girls, "Help yourselves to another piece of cake if you would like." Before she was out of the kitchen she saw them cutting into the cake.

She rushed across the dining room to the living room where there was another phone on an end table next to her sofa. With trembling fingers she dialed Plumstead Township Police Headquarters once again. When a woman answered the phone Hattie asked for Lt. Jim Sawyer.

As she had the last time, the woman said that he was on duty but out.

Hattie, more nervous by the minute, tried to keep her voice calm when she asked the woman to please get hold of him as soon as possible. It was truly a matter of life and death. "Please ask him to call me. This is Hattie Farwell, and he knows my number."

The woman was noncommittal, "I'll tell him m'am if I can reach him, but they are all very busy." She sounded bored and tired and not too interested in Hattie's problem.

Desperate, she called the district attorney again.

The D.A. was standing alone in his office staring out of his window at the vicious storm. He had sent Carolyn and the detectives home, and now he was the only person left in the courthouse with the exception of the guards on the first floor.

The chief of the Plumstead Township Police had just returned his call. He realized the urgency of Allen's problem he said, but his men were tied up with the storm, and he didn't know how any of them could make it to the Atkins' house.

Allen was extremely uneasy. "Please be sure to get someone over there as soon as possible. I have no doubt that the killer, Mahlon Everly, is in that house with Mrs. Atkins, and no one else is there. Her life is in serious danger. I'll do everything I can to help, but she desperately needs police assistance."

"Yes, sir," said the chief, "I'll do my best."

When Hattie's frightened call came through Allen felt terrible that he had nothing to tell her except that they were trying to get help to Donna as soon as possible. "Believe me, we're working on it," he assured her.

Hattie decided at that point the only thing left for her to do was to pray.

chapter twenty-five

olf ran rapidly through the patio doors and across the family room. He sniffed the floor until he picked up Everly's scent at the top of the cellar stairs. Without hesitation he ran down them at once.

Donna watched the dog disappear from her sight as she pushed snow outside between the glass doors, shoved them shut but failed to lock them. What was the point? Everly was already in the house. With her heart racing she followed the dog as far as the top of the stairs.

She caught her breath in renewed terror when she looked down at the spot where Everly had fallen. HE WAS NOT THERE!

Wolf, with his hackles up, ran across the basement barking and snarling viciously.

Donna hesitated briefly before she took her courage in her hands and crept cautiously down the stairs.

Trembling, she leaned over the railing and looked toward Wolf. Everly was nowhere in sight, but the great dog was carrying on outside the closed door to the laundry. His hackles were now raised to the degree that his whole spine seemed elevated. His lips were curled back in a vicious snarl.

Inside the laundry room Everly picked up the hatchet which he had dropped on the floor earlier in the day. He knew the dog would have to die before he could get to Donna.

Upstairs again Donna hurriedly slammed and locked the cellar door shut and at the same time slid a brass bolt into place. She truly believed that Wolf would keep Everly trapped in the laundry room until help arrived, but she was not about to take any chances. Everly was a mad man.

She was convinced that Everly would not be able to climb through the small high window in the back of the laundry. Even if he did, he would have to dig through several feet of heavy snow beyond it. She discarded that thought — it just wasn't possible.

With Wolf's persistent growling and barking ringing in her ears, Donna dashed to the front door, unlocked and opened it. Despite the roof over the porch, the snow was piled high against the storm door, making it impossible for her to push it open.

The snow appeared to be falling faster than ever. She could not make out anything under its white blanket. Bushes and shrubs had been transformed into barely discernible lumps, and the road could not be identified because of the drifts.

She closed the door, leaving it and the storm door unlocked. Spinning on her heel she turned and raced back to the family room and the door to the garage. She had no idea where she would go if she got out, but she just had to get out. Could she possibly make it to Hattie's?

Wolf's angry snarls were the only sounds coming from the basement.

Hurriedly she opened the door and stepped into the garage, which despite the warmth of the house, was bitter cold. She grabbed a jacket from the hook next to her wet coat, but it did little to ward off the chill.

Shivering as much from panic as from the frigid air, she pressed the button to open the outside garage doors. The doors clicked and groaned, but nothing happened. She tried again and again but to no avail.

Returning to the family room, she shut the door into the garage, and as she had with the others, left it unlocked. Once again she ran to the patio doors and with some difficulty slid one of them open about a foot. The icy snow stood straight up in the opening even without the door to lean on.

Wolf's barking and snarling had increased in intensity.

Donna ran to the coat closet where she pulled on high boots, shrugged into a heavy jacket with a hood. Found a pair of warm mittens and put them on. Returning to the sliding doors, she pushed herself through the small opening.

Sleet and snow stung her face the instant she went outside. She stepped down onto the patio and realized that the depth of the snow was well above her knees and still piling up.

She struggled away from the house, but she could barely walk. She realized she could not plow her way through the heavy snow, so she tried to lift her legs and move them ahead just a few inches each time, but that didn't work, and she tripped and fell forward.

With difficulty she pulled herself upright and began to make her agonizing way back to the house. She was breathless and exhausted. "I'm trapped," she thought in terror.

Suddenly she noticed the snow caving in above the window well by the laundry.

"Ohmigosh!" she cried, "Everly's got the window open, and he's trying to come out!"

She tried to increase her pace across the patio and fell forward into the heavy snow once again. In a complete panic she struggled desperately until she finally regained her footing.

Floundering, unable to hurry, she slowly made her way back toward the doors. As she did she kept watching the snow over the window well as it continued to cave in. Finally it stopped. Was he resting? Had he given up? Was he about to start digging his way out again like a crab in the sand?

With her heart threatening to pound its way out of her chest, she inched her way closer to the house. Snowflakes pelted her face and froze on her eyelashes. She could barely see. Tears froze on her cheeks.

At last, breathless, she reached the patio doors. In her terror she had neglected to close the door through which she had left, and snow was piling up inside.

Now the door, jammed with ice, would not close. What if Everly climbed out through the laundry window? He would just come in through that door!

Donna shivered again. Then without removing her coat or boots she took a brass fireplace shovel and began to chip away at the ice.

Wolf was still barking in the cellar.

The ice seemed to form faster than it chipped, and after an extra hearty chop, Donna bent the handle of the shovel and ruined it. Throwing it aside in frustration she returned to the fireplace and grabbed the poker.

Her luck was better in breaking away the ice with the poker, and she had almost finished her task when Wolf began to growl and snarl more furiously than ever.

The ice finally dispensed with, she closed the door, locked it to its mate and with her foot, pressed down the locks behind each door. "Now he won't get in here she exclaimed with satisfaction. Then she removed her jacket and boots.

Perhaps it would be wise to lock the front door, too, she decided. She was turning to do just that when Wolf's snarling and growling became even more ferocious. Then abruptly he emitted a loud and pitiful yelp followed by a low moan.

Donna screamed. She ran to the cellar door to listen for Wolf, but there was nothing but silence. Then she heard Mahlon Everly's hideous laugh preceded by a vengeful, "That will shut you up, you lousy mutt!"

"Oh, no!" Donna whispered in tears, "What did he do to Wolf? He didn't kill him, did he? Oh, Lord, please don't let Wolf be dead!"

She had no time to think or to plan her next action. Everly was jiggling the knob of the cellar door. She looked around desperately. Where could she go to hide?

The garage, she thought, and immediately she ran across to the door grabbing the keys from the counter as she went.

She had barely opened the garage door when the hatchet blade came through the cellar door! She leapt into the garage and was just closing the door when the hatchet blade crashed through the cellar door again! With shaking fingers she locked the deadbolt on the garage door with a key.

The crashing continued until Donna heard Everly slip open the bolt on the cellar door and walk into the family room. "Where are you, Donna?" he called in saccharine sweet tones, "I'm coming to get you! You can't hide from me too long."

She heard his footsteps fade and figured he was either in the hall or dining room. "Oh, Donna!" His voice seemed to be coming from the hall. She crept silently to the far side of the garage and stood between the car and the wall.

She thought of hiding inside the car and locking all of the doors, but she was certain that he would smash his way in to her.

After what seemed like ages, Donna heard him at the door to the garage. She squatted down beside the car and was surprised to see that she was still holding the poker.

Her terror was so great that all she could concentrate on was the door. Suddenly she realized that she was holding her breath and forced herself to breathe slowly.

chapter twenty-six

*T*he district attorney had barely moved since he and Hattie had terminated their brief phone call. He was a man used to being in control, and now he felt he could do nothing to save the life of the poor young woman trapped in her house with Mahlon Everly.

He sat at his desk and placed his head in his hands. He wanted to cry. His colleagues knew him as a compassionate individual who really cared about other people. He often went out of his way to help a person in need, going far beyond the call to duty.

And now the worst crime of all might be taking place as he sat at his desk, and there was nothing he cold do about it. In total frustration he rose from his desk chair and walked back to the window.

He felt as though he had been spending hours looking out of

this window, and the only thing that changed was the depth of the rapidly accumulating snow. There was no motion on the street below, no one driving or walking. Just nothing. An arctic wasteland, he thought.

He phoned home and found to his relief that his wife and two children were all there. He told his wife that he didn't know when or how he would be home, but he was safe, warm and dry, and he could buy food from the vending machines on the first floor if he got hungry.

Sleep was out of the question.

Frozen snowflakes pelted his window, and the wind velocity increased. He couldn't take his thoughts away from the poor girl trapped with that vicious killer. What was she doing? What was she thinking? Was she still alive? What was he doing?

What can I do? There has to be something I can do. Think, think, think. He grit his teeth and ran his hands through his thinning hair. What, what, what can I do?

Once more he returned to the window. The snow was falling faster than ever, whirling, blowing, piling up below. The roofs of the beautiful old Victorian homes across the street were so deep in snow that they looked like iced cakes in a story book.

He stared above the frosted roofs as if he could see into the distance. That's where Donna Atkins' house is. Way off there, about 9 miles straight ahead. Oh to be able to penetrate that storm!

He knew that no one could get to Donna, even the police, who were so busy now with cars and people stranded in the snow. Although the Plumsteadville Police Chief didn't come out and state it, the police officers were no doubt stranded themselves in this storm — the worst blizzard in over a century.

The D.A.'s thoughts were dismal. He believed that he was the one to save Donna, but how? He closed his eyes and strained his brain.

As he had done in brain storming sessions in law school, he tried to think of any way Donna could be saved — even silly ways, such as flying a helicopter over. "Oh really!" he said aloud to himself.

chapter twenty-seven

Everly tried to open the door. "Hah, Donna!" he yelled, "I do believe I have found you! Get ready, I'm coming to put you away, hah hah!

Bile rose in her throat. She began to shake uncontrollably, but she remained hidden in her spot.

A loud crash and the hatchet blade came through the garage door. The thought of the hatchet made her gag. She had no doubt that he had used it on poor, brave Wolf.

Another crash and another. This door was sturdier than the other. Finally he reached in and futilely attempted to unlock the door. In exasperation he threw his great weight against the door and cracked what was left of it away from the frame.

Donna's grip on the poker tightened. She crouched next to the rear wheel and looked under the car to see where he was going.

To her complete horror, she saw him looking back at her from the other side of the car! Again he laughed his maniacal laugh.

She felt as if she were looking at him through a magnifying glass. Every detail stood out in sharp relief.

He was leaning on his right hand, the axe on the floor beneath it. There was blood on the axe, and there was also blood dripping down his left arm onto his hand. In that brief moment when she looked at him, she also realized that he was not putting any of his weight on his left hand.

Donna shuddered violently. There was no thinking to be done now. No plotting. She just had to wait for him to make the next move.

Abruptly he pushed himself to his feet. Still on her knees, Donna saw him start running toward the rear of the car.

She jumped up, and in a crouched position, hoping to remain out of his sight she ran toward the front. The poker was still clutched tightly in her right hand.

Before she rounded the vehicle, he was bearing down on her from the rear on her side of the car.

Breathlessly she continued around to the other side. Everly gained on her with every step. She glanced quickly at the shattered door to the family room but realized there was not enough time for her to maneuver through the splintered wood.

She had raced almost to the back of the car when he caught up to her. She screamed and heard her scream echo back at her from the bare walls as she spun to face him.

His left arm hung limply at his side. The sleeve was torn to shreds and blood was dripping from numerous wounds from his shoulder to his hand.

He must have been in pain , but he showed no sign of it. An evil grin spread over his face when he saw her staring at his useless arm.

"That damn dog will never bite anyone again!" he snarled, "and next it's your turn!"

He grabbed her with his right hand as he spoke, "But before I kill you, I want to look at you again — like I did the day your husband was feeling your treasures in front of the glass doors! You looked real good, Donna, real sexy,"

He began to tear at her sweater, "You know, Donna, you're a good looking woman. Why shouldn't we have some fun before I kill you? We've got lots of time. It's still snowing like Hell out there."

"No, no, no!" Donna screamed, "Let me go!'

"No, no, no, baby," he laughed, and he tugged harder at her sweater until he had pulled it from her body.

He was still able to overpower her with only one good arm, and she was more terrified than ever. Now she was down to her bra, and he was looking at her with increasing excitement. "Why should I hang around here with a corpse until the storm stops?" he asked in reasonable tones, and he reached for the waist of her slacks.

She freed herself from him just enough to swing the poker at his left shoulder. He swore in pain and rage at the impact and raised the bloody hatchet with his right hand.

"O.K. baby, have it your way," he snarled, his pale eyes full of vengeance. She tried to break free, but he pinned her against the car's fender with his body.

Her total concentration was on the blade of the hatchet above his head. Again she swung the poker at him with more strength than she knew she had. The poker struck his damaged left forearm and broke more skin. Blood spurted from the wound.

He yelled in pain and backed a few feet away from the swinging weapon.

Suddenly he swung the hatchet at the poker, jerking it from Donna's hand and sending it spinning across the floor.

He raised the hatchet once again and lunged toward Donna when an earsplitting blast reverberated through the garage.

The hatchet fell harmlessly to the floor as Everly's head jerked forward and his huge body staggered against Donna, crushing her against the car.

His face was horrible. A bright red hole had opened in the center of his forehead, and blood and serum oozed from his eyes, nose and mouth. Donna screamed once more as his body slumped down hers and crumpled in a heap on the floor at her feet.

She looked across Everly's corpse to the family room door where Jim Sawyer was just stepping into the garage through the broken frame. He held his smoking gun in his hand.

chapter twenty-eight

An hour later Donna, wrapped in a blanket, was sitting in the reclining chair in the family room. Her feet were elevated and a pillow supported her head. She was sipping a cup of strong tea.

Hovering next to her was a paramedic from the local volunteer ambulance corps. The name Sharon was machine stitched in white on her blue uniform.

The district attorney sat in a chair to her right and was slowly and gently asking her questions about her nightmarish ordeal. Before she answered any of his questions she had a very important one to ask him, "How did you all get here in this blizzard?"

He told her, "I commandeered a snowplow in Doylestown, and in it the driver and I led two police cars and an ambulance through the snowy roads to your house. It was not easy, believe me," he said, "but I couldn't think of another thing to do. I was desperate."

"When we got here we all grabbed shovels from the back of the truck and cleared the path to your front door — just in the nick of time. We heard your scream coming from the garage. Thank God your front door was unlocked."

Donna was still shivering. Her first action as soon as she got out of the garage had been to go to Wolf. Jim had run down the cellar steps ahead of her and warned her not to follow, but she did, anyway, not mindful of the way she was dressed.

They had found Wolf lying motionless on the floor near the laundry door, his head in a pool of blood. Jim had knelt over him, and Donna had burst into tears.

"He's breathing!" Jim had told her, "Who is his vet? We'd better call him quick."

He had run up the cellar stairs and picked up the phone before the district attorney stopped him, "Everly cut her phone wires," he said, "Here use my cell phone."

Someone took one of Donna's jackets from the hall closet and helped her into it. The pressure of the material on her damaged left shoulder made her wince in pain.

""Here," said Sharon the paramedic, "come upstairs with me and let me tend to that."

"No, not yet. I've got to see about Wolf." Donna answered.

While Donna gave Jim the phone number of the veterinary clinic, the D.A. enlisted another paramedic from the ambulance crew to see what he could do for Wolf.

"You understand, Mr. Allen," the medic said, "I'm not too familiar with animals, but it looks as if the hatchet grazed his skull and almost severed his left ear. He seems to have lost a lot of blood, but I can stop that until he sees the vet." The dog hadn't moved.

Sharon had attached herself to Donna insisting that she go to the second floor with her so she could look her over, "I think you should go to the hospital," she said, but Donna remained adamant, "As I told you before, I can't leave until I know about Wolf, and I don't want to go to the hospital."

There was no doctor available, of course, to pronounce Everly dead, so his body could not be moved until the coroner came. Three police officers were in the garage, and since there was little for the ambulance crew to do when Donna refused to go to the hospital, the D.A. suggested that the men take Wolf to the veterinary hospital.

Donna and Sharon stood at the top of the cellar stairs and watched the men bring Wolf's still form up on a litter, down the hall and out the front door to the waiting ambulance. "This surely is a first! This must be some dog," one of the men said, and Donna answered, "You don't know the half of it. That dog is a hero!"

She called Hattie on the D.A.'s cell phone, and when she heard her voice she burst into tears. She told her about everything, and then she told her about Wolf, "They think he'll be O.K., thank goodness," she said. After she said a quick, "hi" to each of the girls, she hung up and Sharon finally took her upstairs.

While they were gone, Allen started a fire in the family room fireplace. Sharon found Donna's vital signs to be within normal limits, although her blood pressure was low.

She treated and bandaged the scrapes on Donna's left arm and helped her into a clean blouse and sweater before they returned to the family room.

Sitting with the fire, blanket and tea to warm her, Donna began to relax a little. Allen's voice was soothing and Sharon's and Jim's presence were comforting. She found herself dozing a little.

Allen's voice startled her, "Donna, it's six o'clock. Would you like to call your husband?"

Ben answered the phone on the first ring. His relief when he heard Donna's voice was apparent, but the story she told him was worse than his most frightening fears "I'll leave as soon as the roads are passable," he declared, "I'll be home before you know it!" Donna began to sob, "Just drive carefully," she sniffed.

The district attorney looked at her carefully after she had hung up. "We won't be able to stay too much longer," he said, "I can't leave you here alone. Is there anyone you would like to have come over?"

"Hattie Farwell," she said in a small voice, "but can't I go to her? I don't think I can stay here the way it is. I don't know if I'll ever be able to live here again. I felt so secure and safe here, and now that's changed."

"I understand," he said, "I'll have Jim take you over as soon as he can."

The ambulance crew came back with the coroner a little over an hour later.

"Wolf's in the operating room, and Dr. Jensen, his vet, said he's going to be just fine."

"Oh, thank heaven!" Donna sobbed,, "I'll call Hattie right away with the good news if I many use your cell phone again, Mr. Allen."

When Donna told Hattie the good news about Wolf, Hattie cried, too. Then Donna told her that Jim would bring her over, and Hattie was delighted.

Before the doctor pronounced Mahlon Everly dead he gave Donna a quick examination. "It's not often I look at living people," he said with a kind smile. He turned to Sharon, "You did an excellent job with this arm," he told the beaming young woman.

To Donna he said, "Your blood pressure is too low, but that's to be expected, "Make an appointment with your doctor tomorrow, and get a prescription for sleeping pills."

"You, too," he advised Jim, "You had no choice but to kill that man, but you are going to have a hard time with it for a while. It's important for both of you to get your sleep." As he walked into the garage he added, "It wouldn't hurt either of you to get some psychological counseling, too."

Donna turned to Jim, "How do I thank someone who saved my life?"

He gave her a wan smile and said, "I often wondered what I'd do if I had to kill someone. As it turned out, I really didn't have time to think about it when I saw him going at you with that hatchet.

"Now, though, it's making me sick. I blew a hole right through a man's head!" He was silent for a moment before he turned and followed the doctor into the garage.

Not long afterward Everly's body was taken to the ambulance

for its trip to the morgue, and everyone started to leave.

"I'll just tack up a sheet of plywood over this doorway before we leave for Hattie's," Jim told her as he carried the plywood in from the garage.

"I called the phone company when you were upstairs, "Allen said, "They'll be out tomorrow as soon as possible to repair your cut wires. I also phoned a carpenter friend of mine. He'll be here tomorrow to see about your doors and anything else which needs repairing.. I hope that's O.K.

"Oh yes," she answered, "I can't thank you enough for everything you have done,"

The district attorney smiled at her with great sympathy, "No thanks needed. Now I suggest that you phone your homeowners insurance agent as soon as you can."

He started out the door, "Look!" he exclaimed, "the snow has stopped! Pretty soon everything will be back the same as always."

"No," Donna said under her breath, "Nothing will ever be the same again."

the end

Printed in the United States
1359100006B/61-85